"Stop! Police! Let her go!"

Jacob aimed high and fired. The criminal froze like an animal caught in headlights. But Grace didn't stop for a second. She spun back with her elbows high and struck Cutter in the face. The criminal bellowed and grabbed his nose. She broke free and pelted down the rock face toward Jacob.

"Jacob!" she shouted. "He's got a semiautomatic! He just needs to reload!"

He ran toward her, reaching the rock face just as she reached the edge. She looked down. "How do I get down from here?"

"Jump! I'll catch you!"

Her eyes scanned the drop, and then her chin rose. "Okay. I'm coming!"

He shoved his gun back in his holster. She took a deep breath and leaped.

But even as she jumped, Jacob saw the stocky figure of one of the convicts ahead, a fresh gun clutched in his hand. His heart stopped.

He had one convict ahead of them, one behind them, a forest to his right, a rock wall to his left...and a woman he had to protect with his life.

Maggie K. Black is an award-winning journalist and romantic suspense author with an insatiable love of traveling the world. She has lived in the American South, Europe and the Middle East. She now makes her home in Canada with her history-teacher husband, their two beautiful girls and a small but mighty dog. Maggie enjoys connecting with her readers at maggiekblack.com.

Books by Maggie K. Black

Love Inspired Suspense

True North Heroes

Undercover Holiday Fiancée
The Littlest Target
Rescuing His Secret Child
Cold Case Secrets

Amish Witness Protection

Amish Hideout

Military K-9 Unit

Standing Fast

True North Bodyguards

Kidnapped at Christmas
Rescue at Cedar Lake
Protective Measures

Visit the Author Profile page at Harlequin.com for more titles.

COLD CASE SECRETS

MAGGIE K. BLACK

HARLEQUIN® LOVE INSPIRED® SUSPENSE

Recycling programs for this product may not exist in your area.

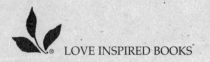

LOVE INSPIRED BOOKS

ISBN-13: 978-1-335-23221-2

Cold Case Secrets

Copyright © 2019 by Mags Storey

www.Harlequin.com

Printed in U.S.A.

For I knew that thou art a gracious God,
and merciful, slow to anger, and of great kindness,
and repentest thee of the evil.
–*Jonah* 4:2b

With thanks to Constable Eran Schwartz
for showing me around his helicopter, training with me
at the dojo and answering countless questions.
You are a shining example of the kind of person
all those in law enforcement should be. Thanks to
Pastor Josh Darsaut for the Bible verse and your
unexpected grace on a rough day. Thanks as always to
my agent, Melissa Jeglinski, and editor, Emily Rodmell,
for your help and support on this journey. And finally,
thanks to all of you who were there for me while I was
writing this difficult book. I hope you enjoy it.

ONE

The thrumming of the helicopter rotors were like a steady drum beat pounding through Jacob Henry's mind as the Royal Canadian Mounted Police detective scanned the monitor for any sign of life in the dense Ontario forest below. Outside the cockpit window, the summer sun was just beginning its descent behind thick and oppressive clouds. Silvery outlines of opal raindrops traced streaks down the windshield. Tense words between the young Search and Rescue pilot sitting beside him and the testy East Coast detective in the back seat filled his headset.

"I'm just saying that when the wind picks up and the rain hits for real, we're going to be forced to turn back," the pilot, Kevin Faust, said. "I don't want to crash."

"And I'm just saying when you've flown as many flights as I have, you know what you can get away with," Detective Warren Scott shot back.

"As a hobby pilot," Kevin said. "Not a professional with Search and Rescue."

Jacob focused on the black-and-white screen ahead of him, searching for the bright glare of a human heat signature.

Wherever the escaped convicts are, Lord, and whoever ultimately finds them, please may those killers be recaptured tonight.

Authorities were scrambling across Ontario to find three convicted killers who'd overpowered their guards and forced the prison van transporting them to crash on the Trans-Canada Highway almost twenty miles north of the maze of trees and towering rocks that made up Algonquin Provincial Park. While local police searched nearby towns and buildings, and provincial police checked the roads, Jacob and Warren had volunteered for the aerial search of the almost three-thousand-square mile provincial park. Home to over two thousand lakes and seven-hundred-and-fifty miles of river, it was a haven for the kind of off-the-grid campers who enjoyed hiking and canoeing for days into the middle of nowhere.

They might as well have been searching for a quarter in a cornfield.

"They're probably not even out here," Kevin argued, speaking into his headset microphone to be heard over the sound of the rotors. "If I'd just escaped a concrete box, the last place I'd be hiding out is somewhere with no running water or electricity."

Maybe not. But moments ago, there'd been a blip, a heat signature, that had lit up the screen for a fleeting moment like a beacon. They just had to find it again.

Jacob focused on the infrared monitor. "Just give me five."

"You can have a whole twenty," Kevin said, "if the rain doesn't get worse before then. But in twenty minutes I'm turning around, one way or another, because otherwise we're running out of fuel."

"Heard that." Jacob's eyes didn't flicker from the screen.

Lord, help me see what I need to see.

Nothing but his own pale face reflected back at him, reminding him of an entire summer spent indoors, reading evidence on screens. The light brown scruff that brushed his jaw was more from lack of shaving than intention and tinged with a bit more white than he liked admitting.

"I just don't want to head back with nothing," Warren said, then muttered, almost as if to himself, "I gave up a date for this."

Jacob cut his eyes in the detective's direction. He'd vaguely known Warren from their large regional high school, before the other man had moved out east for college, so he knew he was also getting close to forty. Warren had only transferred back to Ontario in the spring and already he was dating? How did people even date now? Where did they even meet? Jacob couldn't remember the last time he himself had so much as gone out with anyone for coffee. At two years away from the big four-oh himself, Jacob had been in the business of stopping killers long enough to know that saving other people's lives and having a life of your own didn't mesh. Despite the fact that Jacob's three younger brothers had recently all decided to prove him wrong.

"I gave up bowling with my league," Kevin offered, with a grin that implied the twentysomething was trying to lighten the mood in their hovering box. "Canadian-style. Five pin."

Well, guys, I've risked missing something way more important than that.

The words crossed his mind, but he had enough self-control not to say them out loud. He didn't know either man well enough to confide in them and some things just cut too deep to say without thinking. It had been just over twenty-four years since his little sister, Faith, had been snatched off the side of a rural road at the age of twelve and died fighting off her attacker. Jacob had been fourteen, the eldest child and the one who was supposed to look out for his siblings. And while, over the years, his brothers had each found their own ways to make peace with the memory of their sister, for Jacob, Faith's face was always there, like a picture he'd taped to the corner of his mind's eye, reminding him of the one killer he had yet to catch. Then recently a fellow detective under very deep cover, named Liam Bear-smith, had reached out to say he'd found a fresh lead in Faith's case and was willing to risk both his cover and his life to pass that information onto Jacob. They were supposed to meet at a highway coffee shop at midnight, after Jacob went to his brother Trent's bachelor party.

And I'm here with you two scanning trees. But he caught his griping before it could grow and instead channeled it into prayer. *Lord, please resolve this soon. May the three convicts be caught, help me get back to base in time to meet up with Liam and help me get the information I need to put my sister's killer away for good.*

"It takes days to walk or canoe across the park," Warren said. "I know they shut the park down, but it's possible there could still be campers out there who have no idea there are convicts on the loose. Let alone a serial predator like Barry Cutter who murdered five women, including two ex-girlfriends. Or Victor Driver who went around starting bar fights that put people into the hospital before beating his ex's new husband to death and her brother into a coma. Or Hal Turner."

Kevin shuttered. Jacob noted Warren didn't bother to give Hal Turner's crime résumé. There was no need. The dirty cop turned cop killer was notorious in law enforcement for having killed both his partner and an informant. He'd then tried to burn down a building to destroy the evidence of his thriving drug business and claimed he'd been set up by rogue cops.

Even though Jacob had been a teenager at the time, he'd known even then that God was calling him to a life in law enforcement. Here Turner had achieved everything professionally that Jacob was both hoping and striving for, only to then turn around and betray his brothers and sisters in blue, damage their reputation and give dozens of criminals grounds for appeal.

"I get it, we're hunting bad guys," Kevin said. "But that doesn't change the weather or how much fuel we've got."

A small building passed through the frame. It was a ranger cabin by the looks of it. There were a handful of small and very rustic cabins dotted around the expansive park that had been build back in the 1930s to serve some long-abandoned purpose like storage or lookout. Bare bones, with no electricity or running water, they still wouldn't make for a half-bad hideout, if a person were able to find one.

A bright patch blinked onto the screen near the building. Jacob sat up straight, as he felt the sudden jolt of shock, surprise and relief combined. "We have a heat signature!"

"Please tell me it's not another bear—" Warren started.

"No, it's a person," Jacob said. He heard Kevin whistle, but his eyes stayed locked on the screen. The figure was definitely human and female by the looks of it, willowy and slender with long hair and just the hint of curves visible through her jeans and survival jacket. "A woman."

"Out there alone?" Kevin asked. Jacob glanced at him just long enough to see the flicker of worry cross his face. "In the middle of nowhere? Why didn't we see her earlier?"

Jacob watched as she crept along a tall rock face that ran like a jagged uneven wall between thick trees on one side and a raging river on the other.

"Camera range isn't that broad," Jacob said. "She could've been in a cave, or there are some pretty big rock outcroppings that could've hidden her heat signature."

Kevin's finger jabbed at Jacob's screen as a second larger figure stepped into the frame. "She's not alone."

Yeah, and judging by the way she was creeping along the rock face, that wasn't a good thing. The second heat signature was large, heavyset and barging through the trees. The outline of his jacket did little to hide the telltale shape of a baggy prison jumpsuit or the handgun in his grasp.

"We've got to get down there!" Jacob said.

"There's nowhere to land!" Kevin's voice rose.

"It's one of them!" Jacob said. "It's a lifer. He's going to kill her!"

"I know! I just can't land!"

They watched, helpless, as the man chased after her, tackled her and brought her to the ground. Something lurched in Jacob's core as if he were somehow viscerally able to hear her terrified screams. She thrashed and fought back hard. And Jacob realized, for the first time in his life, he was about to watch a woman's murder. He yanked his seat belt off, pushed himself out of his seat and climbed into the back of the helicopter. "Warren, get into the front and take over for me. I'm going to rappel down."

"From this height?" Warren asked. "In the rain? Are you trying to get yourself killed?"

Yes, yes and hopefully not. Jacob slid his arms through a safety harness and didn't answer. He glanced back at the screen and his heart soared momentarily to see the figures had broken apart. *Lord, just help her stay alive until I can get there.*

"I'm going to need you to lower me down," Jacob said. He double-checked his walkie-talkie, phone and his service gun were all on his belt. "Rappel rope is fine. Though I'm suggesting you use the rescue ladder or basket to pull us back up. For now, just get me as close as you can, stay in my ear and point me in the right direction."

"It should be me," Warren started. "You're the one on infrared."

Maybe, but Jacob was also the one who'd gotten his harness on first.

"There's still a storm coming—" Kevin's face was awash with fear "—and I'm still really low on fuel."

Right. That twenty minutes was probably closer to fifteen by now.

"We'll figure it out!" Jacob double-checked his clasps and opened the door. Wind and rain lashed at him. A deep breath of confidence filled his lungs. Nobody was ever going to die at a criminal's hands as long as he had something to say about it. He cast one final glance at the outline of the woman below, now pelting through the trees with her attacker close on her heels.

Stay strong. Don't give up. I'm coming for you.

The blow from behind came so hard and suddenly that Grace Finch felt the air knocked from her lungs even before she hit the ground. For a moment, her body's own natural instinct to freeze threatened to overwhelm her. Then she reared, kicking up hard with both legs and felt herself break free. She rolled and tried to get her feet beneath her before a swift punch to the temple knocked her back against the ground.

The blunt and scarred face of Barry Cutter glared down at her, and Grace felt his entire rap sheet flash through her mind, just as clearly as if she'd been sitting at her crime reporter desk at *Torchlight News*, reading his bio in her news files. Bartholomew "Barry" Cutter, age fifty-four, convicted to fifty years in prison for the brutal murders of five women.

Help me! Someone! Anyone! Please!

A large hand with thick fingers grabbed her by the throat and pushed her down. The semi-automatic SIG he waved between her eyes looked police-issued. And suddenly she felt the journalist inside her wanting to ask him how he'd gotten there, what he was doing out of prison and if it had anything to do with the Search and Rescue helicopter she'd seen flying overhead. There was a major news story here, if she got out of here alive to tell it. She swallowed a breath and reminded herself that if Cutter wanted her dead, he'd have killed her by now. Then slowly she began to slide her right hand toward the stun gun in her jacket pocket.

"Where's your car?" Cutter snapped. She felt her mind filtering out the threats and curses that peppered his voice, listening only for facts. "Take me to your car. Now! You're driving me out of here!"

Didn't he know where they were? Night was falling, and she'd spent the better part of the day getting this deep into the woods. Her car was at the entrance to the park, at least six hours of canoeing and portaging away. For that matter, how had he even gotten here?

As for her, she'd been coerced here, lured here, out into the middle of nowhere by another convicted killer, Hal Turner, on the promise of finding information that would clear him of his crimes, prove he'd been set up by some shadowy cabal of senior cops and free Grace of the specter of blackmail he'd been holding over her life. Ever since she had risen as a star crime reporter, Turner had been blackmailing her and threatening to destroy her life and career by telling the world a truth she'd spent her entire life concealing.

That Grace Finch was really Hal Turner's biological daughter.

That the country's most prolific and award-winning

crime reporter was really the child of the so-called dirty cop turned cop killer.

In her business, reputation was everything. Her biological father was one of the most hated convicted killers in the country, especially as far as those in law enforcement were concerned. What if sources refused to talk to her because of who her father was? What if someone with a grudge against Turner decided to come after her? After all, he'd not only betrayed his badge and worked with organized crime, he'd then besmirched all of law enforcement with wild stories of a deep-seated conspiracy of criminal cops. No evidence had ever been found to back up his claims. What if she was fired from her job at *Torchlight News* and blackballed from the industry for keeping the truth about her identity secret? Even if Turner was somehow right—he had been set up by someone, and this evidence he'd sent Grace to find would prove it—how would anyone in her life ever trust her again for keeping her identity secret so long?

Let alone forgive her.

No, she'd worked too long and hard to build a life on her own terms to let it all be taken from her now.

Not to mention her incredibly strong mother, and Mom's kindhearted husband, Frank, who'd raised Grace as his own, both deserved better than to have their lives dragged through the mud.

So she'd hiked and paddled into the woods in search of a secluded cabin where he'd claimed to have left evidence proving his innocence. It was a simple transaction. She'd publish the evidence, his lawyer and the courts would do their thing, Hal Turner would keep his mouth shut about the daughter no one knew he had and he'd disappear from her life for good.

But she hadn't found the cabin. Instead, a killer had found her.

She'd been desperate. She'd been foolish. And now she was going to die.

Cutter leaned closer, shifting some of his weight off her body. The stench of him filled her nostrils. "Don't fight. Don't scream. We're just going to get in your car and take a nice ride to the American border and then I'm going to let you go."

No, he wouldn't; he'd hurt her and he'd kill her, that much she knew with every fiber of her being. And she'd die fighting before she agreed to take him anywhere.

The helicopter's spotlight flashed above them, dragging her attention to the sky. A figure, tall and broad-shouldered, now dangled from underneath it, suspended from a rope like something out of an action movie. She blinked. Cutter looked up and swore.

It was an unexpected distraction, but she'd take it. Her right hand dove into her jacket pocket, yanked out the stun gun, flicked it on and pressed it hard into his side. Cutter bellowed in pain. The gun fell from his hand. She kicked up, threw him off her and scooped up the gun. Then she stumbled to her feet and ran, pushing and pelting through the branches until she'd lost him in the trees.

The helicopter light swung above her again like a searchlight, filtering through the leaves and illuminating the rock face ahead of her, and that's when she saw the gap. It was narrow, like a slanted alley only about three feet wide. She ran for the gap in the rocks, slid her body inside and pressed herself against the wall. She heard the sound of branches breaking and a voice swearing as Cutter ran by her hiding spot. It was only then she realized her hands were shaking. Hot tears filled her eyes.

God, if You're even still listening to me, thank you so much that I'm still alive! Now, what do I do?

She couldn't remember the last time she'd prayed. But somehow the fear pounding through her had poured out into the need to cry out to the God she'd long stopped talking to for help. She put her stun gun back into her jacket pocket, but kept the gun she'd taken off Cutter clutched tightly in her hand. Could she really shoot and kill a man if it came to it? If his face appeared at the entrance of her hiding place, did she really have what it took to look him in the eyes and pull the trigger?

How much was she really her biological father's daughter?

No, no, she wouldn't let herself think that way. Her father had killed for his own selfish ends, not in self-defense. She was nothing like him. She never had been and never would be.

Her head leaned back against the rock and her eyes closed as she listened to the sounds of the helicopter in the distance, wind brushing the trees, light rain hitting the rocks around her and a river rushing somewhere nearby. Maybe if she could get up to higher ground, she could find a way to signal the helicopter. Maybe she could even spot the cabin, run there and retrieve whatever Turner had left for her. But for now, she was on her own, with a phone that hadn't been able to get a signal in hours and a killer looking for her.

"Grace Miranda Finch!"

Her heart froze mid-beat as suddenly Cutter bellowed her name.

"Senior crime reporter!" His voice grew louder. Twigs snapped and branches cracked. It sounded like he was coming back through the woods, looking for her. "*Torchlight News*, Queen Street, Toronto. Born April third. Age thirty-six."

No! She grabbed her side as if suddenly realizing she was missing an organ. He had her wallet! She hadn't even realized it had fallen from her pocket.

But now he had her life, her address, her identity, he had—

"Hal Turner," Cutter read like a man announcing a public execution, "was convicted today to two consecutive life sentences…"

He had the news clipping she'd cut from the paper at the age of fifteen about her father's conviction and had kept folded small in her wallet ever since as a reminder to never stop working harder, aiming higher and pushing herself to be the best possible person she could be.

"…along with two counts of first-degree murder, drug trafficking, bribery, corruption, breach of public trust…"

Grace tuned Cutter out. She'd obsessively read every article about Turner when he'd first been arrested, hoping with all her heart that no one would ever uncover that the dirty cop had secretly fathered a daughter he barely saw and hardly knew with a twenty-two-year-old emergency room nurse he'd met at a crime scene and never deigned to give either his heart or home to. Turner had bailed long before Grace was born. She'd always had her mother's last name, not his, and while he'd sporadically wanted to see her growing up, had insisted his name not be listed on her birth certificate. She'd never looked like him, not in ways that anybody had noticed, with the slender build and long black hair of her beautiful Afro-Caribbean Canadian mother instead of looking anything like her overweight German Canadian father, whose pale skin was frequently flushed red with anger. No one had ever seemed to suspect she was mixed race, especially after her mom and Frank, a fellow nurse and widower, had drawn close during the pregnancy and married when Grace was two. Gossipmongers speculated that Grace must have always been Frank's, but her mom had consistently risen above others' idle gossip.

But Grace had obsessively followed every moment of the trial. She watched television for hours, flipping through news channels to find his face and then hid in the computer lab when she got into journalism school, scanning the wires for his name. What had she even been looking for? Clues to what would lead a man who'd sworn an oath to protect his community to instead cut deals with drug dealers? Whether there was any credence to the story his lawyer had spun—that his partner had been the real criminal, the deaths had really been a murder suicide and that her father had set the fire in a noble attempt to protect his former partner's name?

She'd been fourteen when he was arrested. She'd been there, in a restaurant-chain coffee shop, wondering why the father she'd barely seen had wanted to see her. His face had been white with fear and his hands had shaken so hard he could barely pick up his coffee cup. Then suddenly six police cars had pulled up outside. He'd leaped to his feet, told her to point the cops in the wrong direction, make up some story about where he'd gone and then quickly get to his apartment, destroy his computer and burn his files. Then he ran, leaving her to watch through the window with a gawking crowd of spectators and journalists as people in uniform chased him down the block. She hadn't talked to the cops or gone to his apartment. Instead, she'd slipped out the back and gone home, the hair prickling at the back of her neck with every step, half expecting a journalist to stop her and ask her what she had been doing with him and who she was. But no one ever had. Seemed that for whatever reason, Turner had actually kept her existence a secret. The next time she saw her father's face was his mug shot on the news.

She hadn't heard from Turner again until she was twenty-eight, when her name was syndicated in newspapers across the country and he needed money.

"Listen to me, Grace Finch, wherever you're hiding!" Cutter shouted, "You looking for Hal Turner? 'Cause I know him. He and I broke out together, and he's real close by. He told me that he was coming here, looking for someone. I can take you right to him. I won't hurt you, I promise."

Her heart stopped. Her father had broken out of prison? Her father was here?

The noise above her was so faint she hadn't even realized someone else was there until the uniformed police officer dropped down into the crevice beside her. Her breath caught in her throat. Her lips parted. But before she could let out a sound, one strong hand clamped over her lips while the other grabbed her hand, closing over the gun and peeling her fingers away from the trigger. The officer pulled her to him so that her back was against his chest.

"It's okay, I've got you." The voice in her ear was strong, warm and compelling, with just a hint of danger, filling her with a sense of reassurance that was as unexpected as it was unfamiliar. "I'm Detective Jacob Henry of the RCMP. I'm here to rescue you, and I'll keep you safe. Do exactly what I say, and I'll get you out of here alive."

TWO

He would, would he? Her relief at knowing she wasn't alone and her irritation at having a man—any man—suddenly announce that he was in charge and all would be well if she just did what he said battled somewhere deep inside her core. Yes, he was a cop. Yes, there was something undeniably and extremely reassuring about the feel of him there. But she'd survived her whole entire life on her own, without ever being rescued by anyone and wasn't about to just fall into anyone's arms now.

Especially not if that someone was Detective Jacob Henry.

Her eyes closed for a moment as the background file she kept on Jacob filled her mind. He'd done more to save lives, rescue others and stop killers than anyone she'd ever known. Not that they'd ever actually met. She'd heard his voice before, usually saying *no comment* and telling her to get off his crime scene before he had her arrested. As for his face, she knew it had a handsome and rugged quality that was a bit rough around the edges, like a former movie star that had retired to build custom motorcycles. But right now, he was holding her too close for her to turn around and see it. She definitely had never let herself imagine what it would be like to be held like this in his arms. Well, at least not in a situation like this.

Jacob Henry had a knack for being the primary detective on practically every major crime scene she'd raced to, especially the worst and more grisly ones. Some veteran detectives—like the immensely charming Warren Scott who'd been supremely friendly since transferring to the Toronto division a few months back—were known to toss reporters like her at least a few scraps of information before politely sending them on their way. But Jacob never had. If anything, he'd avoided even looking at her, let alone making direct eye contact, as if something about her mere existence made him uncomfortable. And maybe it did. Reporters and cops did tend to eye each other warily despite the fact that, as she saw it, they were all on the same team, wanting to see truth win out and bad guys get locked away. She didn't want to know how much worse it would be if he knew she was the daughter of a dirty cop who'd killed a fellow officer.

Of all the cops who could've dropped out of nowhere to rescue her, why oh, why did it have to be him?

In fact, just last week, when she'd heard that her boss's sister, Detective Chloe Brant, was getting married this weekend to Jacob's fellow detective, and brother, Trent, she'd sent Jacob an email, hoping that one point of connection would be enough to thaw the ice between them, enough to grab a friendly and professional off-the-record coffee. Not a date. She definitely hadn't asked him out on a date. Just to grab coffee sometime to see if they could set up a better, less adversarial mode of communication. Instead, he'd ignored her.

Well, he could hardly ignore her now.

And if he didn't get his hand off her mouth pronto, she just might bite him.

He leaned so close she could feel his breath on her face. He smelled like coffee and wood smoke. It was a scent that somehow seemed to match both the toughness and warmth of his voice.

"Hand me the gun," he whispered.

She shook her head. He sighed and twisted it from her grasp so deftly that she had no choice but to let go. He slid it into his ankle holster with one hand and pulled his pant leg down over it. Then his hand was back on her wrist so quickly it almost impressed her.

"Now I'm going to peel my hand away from your mouth," he said. "But I need you to promise not to scream."

Who did this man think she was? No, of course, she wasn't going to scream or start caterwauling with a serial killer lurking nearby. He did know about Cutter, right? That had to be why he was here. Jacob seemed to be waiting for a response, so she nodded definitively and firmly. He eased his hand from her mouth, but the other stayed firm on hers with his fingers brushing just against the inside of her wrist. Yeah, not distracting at all.

"Now," he whispered, "I need you to—"

"Give me my gun back."

Even with her back to him, it was like she could feel his whole body blink.

"Who are you?" His voice sharpened. "Are you law enforcement?"

"I'm Grace Finch, lead crime reporter, *Torchlight News*." She wasn't sure what kind of reaction she was expecting. But it wasn't the stony and awkward silence that filled the space around them. "We've met before. You've ordered me off your crime scenes and ignored my phone calls. I sent you an email about coffee just last week you never responded to."

Okay, so maybe that was a bit testier than she'd intended, but she'd never been one to beat around the bush.

"So you're not law enforcement or the military?" His whisper came back swift and sharp. "Do you have a license to carry a handgun?"

The questions felt rhetorical.

"No, but I've passed the Canadian Firearms Safety—"

"Then it's illegal for you to be carrying a handgun, and you're not getting it back—"

Like she didn't know Canadian gun law. "There's an escaped convict in the woods!"

"Actually, there are three—"

"Three?" She fought and failed to keep her whisper from rising. Did that mean Cutter hadn't lied and her father really had escaped prison? Enough of this. She spun around and turned toward him. Jacob let her go, and then she was facing him, standing so closely she was practically pressed against his chest. She looked up at him in the dying light. His green eyes were serious. His chestnut hair was tousled and spiky with sweat. His face radiated a sense of protection that she didn't even know how to begin to process. "Who are the three convicts?"

"Who did you see?" He deflected her other question with one of his own.

Fine. Sometimes a person had to give information to get information.

"I was attacked by Barry Cutter," she said. "The serial killer. He tried to force me to take him to my car, which is over six hours away by canoe from here. I fought him off and ran."

Jacob let out a long breath and stepped back as far as the narrow space would allow. His voice softened. "How did you possibly get away?"

"I zapped him with a Taser and then took his gun."

He blinked. "That would be the gun I just took from you?"

"Yes," she said.

"Where's the Taser now?"

"In my pocket."

"And did you take that off him too?" Jacob asked.

"No, it's mine."

A faint smile turned at the corner of his mouth. She wondered if he was debating pointing out it was also illegal for her to carry a stun gun.

"He also took my wallet," she added. "And I assume it isn't actually his gun—"

"No, I imagine he took it off a guard." His face turned grim. "About four hours ago, three prisoners overpowered the prison guards who were transporting them. We don't know how it happened yet, but they forced the van to crash and killed the guards. There's a massive manhunt underway across Ontario to find them. I just thank God that I happened to be flying overhead when Cutter attacked you."

Something about the way he said it made her think he actually believed there was a God who had helped him out.

"Was he the only person you saw?" Jacob asked.

"He was," she said.

"Where's Cutter now?"

"I don't know," she said. "But since you dropped down from above me somewhere, I'm guessing it's possible to walk along the top of the rock face. I suggest we climb up, take a look around from there and hail the helicopter. Now, what can you tell me about the other escaped convicts?"

Was Cutter telling the truth? Was her father one of them?

Jacob turned his head away from her. "Henry here." The shift in Jacob's tone was so sudden that it took her a moment to realize he was talking into the shoulder microphone for his walkie-talkie. "I've secured the civilian. She claims to have sighted Barry Cutter. Do you have any other heat signatures in the area?" He paused. "Okay. Heard that."

Maybe he'd heard it, but she was still out of the loop.

"So what's going on? Who are you talking to?"

"That was RCMP SAR pilot, Kevin Faust," Jacob said, and she felt oddly thankful he hadn't felt the need to spell out Royal Canadian Mounted Police Search and Rescue. "Now I need you to stay here and hidden. I'm going to go out there and assess the situation."

"There's nothing to assess. I told you, there's a maniac out there—"

"I wouldn't say maniac—"

"He was convicted of killing two women," she cut him off, "as well as being credibly accused of assaulting several others before then and of killing his own mother."

"And how would you possibly know that?" Jacob asked. "We worked very hard to keep that information out of the public record."

"Because, as I told you, I'm Grace Finch, award-winning crime reporter for *Torchlight News*." Her chin rose. "If you'd ever bothered talking to me or answering my phone calls or emails, you'd know that we don't ever report anything without proper verification, and in some cases authorization. But that doesn't mean we don't know an awful lot more than we let on."

"What are you doing here, Grace?" He shook his head. It was like her mere existence baffled him. "How did you even get here?"

"I hiked and canoed," she said. "It took me six hours. I left my car at the front entrance. I'm heading to a cabin, once I can find it."

"And you honestly had no idea there were escaped convicts on the loose before you decided to come up here?" he asked.

"Absolutely none." Besides, if they had escaped when Jacob had said, she would've already been deep in the forest when they broke out.

"And you just happened to have a Taser on you?" he added.

"Yes," she said. "And bear spray. I'm not in the habit of going places unprotected. Now, who are the other two convicts that escaped?"

"Victor Driver and Hal Turner."

So it was true. Her father had escaped prison. A pain-filled gasp slipped to the edge of her lips, but she slid her hand over them before they made a sound. Jacob looked down at her for a long moment, with an inscrutable look in his eyes that she couldn't begin to make heads or tails of.

"Stay here," he said finally. "Don't move. Don't breathe. Don't make a sound. Once everything is secured, I'll come get you and we'll airlift out of here. Got it?"

"I hear you," she said. "Now, can I please have the gun back?"

"You mean the gun you can't legally carry that you lifted off a criminal?" he asked. "No. Be thankful that I'm choosing to overlook the fact it's also completely illegal for you to have that stun gun."

Yeah, she'd wondered how long he'd be able to go without mentioning that.

"Now stay here," he said again, "and don't do anything stupid. Got it?"

"Got it," she said. "Nothing stupid."

But even then he paused a very long moment with his eyes on her face. "Okay then. We're down to maybe an hour of daylight, if that, and according to my pilot, Kevin, there's a pretty bad storm coming that's probably going to hit sooner than that." Then, as she watched, his gaze rose to the clouds above. "Lord, help me do this. Help get Grace and myself out of here alive. And may somebody catch these killers before anyone gets hurt."

Hang on, had he really just prayed? In front of her? He had, hadn't he?

Jacob unholstered his weapon and slowly moved away from her. She watched as he paused and searched the world outside their hiding place. Then he stepped out and she lost sight of him.

Maybe the fact Jacob had prayed didn't mean anything. She'd heard plenty of people claim to be religious, including a whole lot of criminals just looking for a break at their trial. Yes, Jacob's reputation was impeccable, and maybe there were a few really good people of integrity out there, but she wasn't about to risk her life on Jacob being one.

No, she couldn't risk telling him about the cabin, her father or her real reason for being here. But if she could find the cabin, there was the tiniest possibility she could still retrieve whatever her father wanted her to find before being airlifted to safety.

She cast one last glance through the crevice to the empty space where Jacob had gone and saw nothing but trees. Then she reached up, grabbed hold of a jagged and jutting piece of rock and started climbing.

Jacob stepped into the clearing and paused with his weapon at the ready. It was empty. Water roared far below him to his left. The helicopter whirred above him just out of view. Cutter was nowhere to be seen.

"Hey, Warren, where was the heat signature again?" he asked, his eyes in the sky.

"Ahead about a hundred paces to your left." The detective's voice was back in his headset. "I can track him, but it means losing eyes on the civilian."

Jacob frowned. "Do it."

"Are you sure the man the civilian saw was Barry Cutter?" Now it was Kevin's voice that crackled in his ear.

"Absolutely." He started walking slowly, listening for the sounds of life. He had no doubt in his mind Grace had seen exactly who she'd said. As difficult as that woman was, from what he'd read of her articles, it seemed she was also fairly brilliant and knew her stuff. He took a deep breath and fought the urge to go back and talk to her. Something about the way they'd just left things felt awkward. But what else was there to say? He had an escaped convict to find, a helicopter to catch and an undercover detective to meet up with at midnight to collect new evidence, which would hopefully help him solve the one murder that had been tearing him up inside for over half his life.

And here his brain was having trouble focusing.

Okay, God. Help me do what needs to be done. Help me get my head in the game.

He'd been completely knocked off-kilter, to the point of feeling all of his words fall from his head, the moment Grace had said her name and he'd realized just who he was holding against his chest. Of all the women in the world it could've been, why did it have to be her? Grace Finch was difficult, challenging, a pain in his neck, impossible…and impossibly beautiful with her long legs, bold and determined eyes, and full lips. He'd never known anyone capable of knocking his breath from his lungs by just walking onto a crime scene like her.

Had she really had no idea that three lifers had escaped prison when she'd decided to come camping up here in the middle of nowhere? But how else would she have gotten here in time? The convicts had crashed in a secluded area north of the park, so it made sense they'd been able to travel as deep into the length of the woods as they had in four hours, which is why this was where they'd been searching. But if Grace really had parked at the entrance and hiked in that way, there was no way she could've heard of the prison escape and made it here by now. Not unless she was airlifted in.

But could it really be a coincidence one of the country's best crime reporters just happened to be in the woods in the exact location where notorious serial killers who'd just escaped prison happened to be? Of course not. Not that he could come up with a plausible alternative theory. Or take the time to figure one out now. So much of this didn't make sense. Starting with the fact that his mouth hadn't been able to summon so much as, "Yeah, I know who you are," when she'd told him her name.

He could still remember the first time he'd seen her walking toward him at the crime scene of a multiple homicide, striding right up to the yellow police tape. He'd hoped she was a detective, a colleague, someone he could grab a coffee and talk over cases with. Not that he'd ever considered looking for a romantic relationship with her or anything. He already had enough people who counted on him, what with two elderly parents, three younger brothers—one getting married on the weekend—three new sisters-in-law and two nephews. But he'd never been opposed to building a new professional and collegial friendship.

He also remembered the first time Warren had spotted her at a crime scene. The fellow detective had just arrived back in Ontario earlier after spending over a decade putting away an impressive array of criminal lowlifes out east. And somehow, just a few weeks on the job, she'd already caught his eye.

"That's Grace Finch, the reporter, right?" Warren had nodded in her direction through the maze of flashing red and blue lights punctuating the night. "I heard she's a force and a half."

Jacob couldn't even remember what he'd said next. Maybe, "Yeah, she's pretty tough," or something like that.

"I was thinking of asking her to a new show at the Art Gallery of Ontario," Warren had started saying. Then he'd taken in the look on Jacob's face and added, "Unless for some reason you'd rather I didn't."

And Jacob had realized in that moment just how very much he'd rather Warren didn't. Not that he had any right to ask him not to date Grace. Sure, Jacob had been quick to assure him he had no intention of ever pursuing a relationship with Grace. But that didn't change the fact that he'd been kind of relieved that Warren hadn't either.

He paced a few lengths into the woods, slowly, carefully following the broken branches and disturbed ground that told him someone had gone this way. "Hey, Kevin, how are we doing on the fuel situation?"

"I can give you fifteen minutes." The pilot's voice came back in his ear. "Twenty at the absolute max."

"You said that ten minutes ago."

"Yeah." The sound of Kevin blowing out a hard breath filled his ear. "That was adding in a time cushion just to be safe in case we got delayed by the storm. Now, we're all out of cushion."

"Got it. Warren, have you got eyes on me?"

"Heat signature on your own, moving north?" Warren confirmed. "Yup. But I've momentarily lost the one you were tracking."

Jacob frowned. It happened. The camera's range was not that broad. "How's our civilian doing?"

"Hang on. I've got to move the camera," Warren said. Jacob waited. "I've got no heat signatures near the rock formation. Your civilian is gone. But I think I've got two figures on top of the rock ledge to the east of you."

Jacob turned on his heels. *You have to be kidding me!* Had she actually decided to ignore what he'd said and take off on her own? His strides turned into a full-out sprint. He reached the crevice. It was empty. No Grace. His jaw clenched. "She's gone."

Lord, help me hold it together...

A scream filled the air.

THREE

"Where are they?" Jacob shouted into his headpiece. He ran, pressing his body through the dense woods and keeping his weapon at the ready. The screams had stopped, but his heart was still rattled from the sound. No matter how many bloody crime scenes he'd walked through, grisly photos he'd looked at or difficult interrogations he'd conducted, the one thing that somehow always seemed to slip through the chinks in his cast-iron core and take him right back to being fourteen years old was the sound of someone screaming.

His sister, Faith, had fought for her life. That much he knew without a doubt about the attempted kidnapping that had ended her life. She'd thrashed, kicked and clawed at the would-be abductor. Her killer had strangled her and left her lifeless body there by the side of the road. But he hadn't succeeded in taking her alive. No match had ever been found for the DNA retrieved from under her fingernails. But Jacob had never given up hope that it would and that, one day, he'd would have the satisfaction of knowing that the criminal who'd killed his sister had been sentenced to life in prison because Faith had died fighting him with every ounce of Henry blood pumping through her heart.

Jacob was the one who'd let her down. True, it had been their brother Trent's responsibility to walk Faith home from school. But Jacob was the eldest and he'd been wrong to trust his younger brother to take care of something that important, instead of dropping out of track-and-field to make sure he did it himself. "Warren, tell me you've still got eyes."

"Straight ahead," Warren said. "A bit to your right. You should see them any minute now."

What had he been thinking, leaving Grace alone like that? If she was now on top of the rock face, he imagined that meant she'd somehow climbed up from inside the crevice the moment his back was turned. And then what? And why? What possible reason could she have had for doing that? Did she think she knew better than he did? Grace Finch was more than challenging. She was trouble. And now she was going to get herself killed.

Another scream shook the air. But it wasn't the desperate and panicked cry of a girl in trouble. No, this sound was determined, furious and angry, and something about it lifted his heart.

"Update?" he all but barked.

"Straight ahead!"

Jacob looked up as the trees parted and the top of the ridge he'd been following came into view. There they were, at least a story and a half above him. A bald and heavily tattooed killer named Victor Driver was holding Grace from behind, with one beefy, tattooed arm wrapped around her waist and the other trying to get around her throat. But she was fighting him, thrashing against his grip with all her might.

"Stop! Police! Let her go!" Jacob shouted. He raised his weapon. He'd aim for the shoulder or torso, hopefully taking the man down in a way that kept him alive to face justice. He'd take a kill shot if he had to and only as a last resort. But he didn't have any hope of getting a clear shot as long as Grace was thrashing. Frustration burned inside him. Hadn't she heard him? Didn't she know he was there? If only she would go limp and give him a clean shot, he could save her life. Then it struck him—even if she knew he was there with a gun trained on her attacker, she might still try to take matters into her own hands.

He aimed high and fired. The bullet flew by barely an inch from Driver's head. The criminal froze like an animal caught in the headlights. But Grace didn't stop for a second, almost as if she'd been expecting it. She spun back with her elbows high and struck Driver in the face. The criminal bellowed and grabbed his nose. She broke free and pelted down the rock face toward Jacob.

"Jacob!" she shouted. "He's got a semi-automatic! He just needs to reload!"

He ran toward her, reaching the rock face just as she got to the edge. She looked down. "How do I get down from here?"

"Jump! I'll catch you!"

Her eyes scanned the drop and then her chin rose. "Okay. I'm coming!"

He shoved his gun back in his holster. She took a deep breath and leaped. He opened his arms and she tumbled into them, just as easily and smoothly as if she'd been made to be in them. Her hands latched around his neck. He held her tightly.

Grace Finch was in his arms...

"I'm sorry I left the crevice," she said. "I just wanted to get a better look at what was going on."

"That's okay," he said.

"Thank you for catching me," she said and pushed back against his chest. He set her down. "He's got a modified TEC-9. Don't ask me how because he definitely didn't take that off a guard. All I know is I don't want to be here when he gets it working."

"Me neither." A weapon like that could shred the trees and take them down a dozen times over before they even known what hit them. And a serial killer and escaped convict had somehow gotten ahold of one? "Come on."

Impulsively, he grabbed her hand. She let him take it and together they ran along the rock face.

"Kevin!" he shouted. "We need an airlift. Now."

"Good!" Kevin said. "Because that ten minutes is running out fast."

"Don't remind me," Jacob said. "We had a second criminal sighting—Victor Driver. Somehow he's gotten his hands on a TEC-9."

He could've done without the whistle Kevin filled his ear with.

"How'd he get an illegal black market semi-automatic?" Warren barked. "He must have outside help. There's no way he lifted that from a guard."

"Yeah, we know."

"Are he and Cutter working together?" Warren asked.

"No clue. Just get us out of here, and I'll fill you both in and call in the sightings while we're in the sky."

As much as he'd have liked to bring both Cutter and Driver back with him, saving Grace was enough. More than enough.

"Okay, there's a sheer stretch of rock sixty degrees southeast," Warren said. "I can lower the ladder there. Just follow the sound of the river."

"What about the rescue basket?" Jacob asked.

"There's something wrong with one of the tether points," Warren said. "Ladder is safer."

"Got it," Jacob said. At least he already knew Grace was comfortable climbing, although a suspended ladder wasn't exactly the same as the rock crevice. He ran with Grace by his side and her hand tight in his.

"Watch out!" Kevin said, "There's another heat signature coming up on your right—"

But even as he spoke, he saw the stocky figure of Cutter ahead of them, a fresh gun clutched in his hand. His heart stopped. He had one convict ahead of them, one behind them, a forest to his right, a rock wall to his left...and a woman holding his hand who he had to protect with his life. Jacob pulled his weapon and fired, but not before Cutter was able to get off a shot of his own.

"Grace, get down!" *Save her, Lord!* Jacob leaped, throwing himself in front of Grace just as he felt the searing hot pain of Cutter's bullet pierce his shoulder.

He's been shot! Fear flooded Grace's core, even as her body hit the ground. Jacob landed beside her, his cry of pain mingled with the sound of gunfire that still seemed to echo in the air.

Detective Jacob Henry had been shot.

She rolled, sliding her body out from under him as safely as she could without jolting him. Her eyes darted around the trees. She couldn't see Cutter anywhere, but whether he'd been shot, run off or was just biding his time, he couldn't have gone far. Either way, they couldn't just stay here and wait for him to fire again. A large jagged rock, at least three feet high, lay to her right. She grabbed Jacob's uninjured arm and crawled for it, half leading and half pulling him, feeling him crawl after her. They collapsed behind it and she turned to Jacob. He was lying on his side. Blood seeped from his right shoulder. "Jacob? Are you okay?"

"No!" He groaned. "I've been shot."

She almost laughed at the sheer strength of the frustration in his voice. "Yeah, I got that. Tell me you're left-handed."

"Nope, sorry."

"Do you want me to check it?"

"Not right now. Thankfully it's just a graze." He yanked a bandanna out of his pocket and handed it to her. "Bullet's not in the wound. Tie this down over my arm right here, like a bandage, not like a tourniquet. Hopefully this will absorb the blood and help it clot until we get somewhere we can get it properly bandaged."

She took the bandanna and tied it over his sleeve in the place he pointed. She could tell he was trying not to wince, even through gritted teeth.

"Where are you?" Cutter's voice came from behind the trees. "Get out here! Show yourselves!"

"Sorry, Detective, but I'm borrowing your gun," she said and yanked the weapon from his holster. She crouched on the balls of her feet, set Cutter in her sights and fired twice. He swore and disappeared into the trees. She looked back down. Jacob was saying something in his shoulder microphone.

He looked up. "Tell me you hit him."

"I don't know." She scanned the woods. "But I can't see him or hear him. Driver either. But he can't be far behind. Tell me your guy's ready with that helicopter."

As much as she wanted to reach the cabin and get that information, escaping the shadow of her father's blackmail was way less important than getting them both out alive. Cut bait now. Circle back later.

"Warren says that it looks like Cutter is retreating, Driver's climbing down the rock behind us and that there's a clearing ahead of us to the left. He'll lower the rope down and collect us there." Jacob started to pull himself up, then winced. She reached out her hand for him and felt his hand grip hers for a few moments as he climbed to his feet. Then he let go. "Now give me back my gun."

She bit her tongue to keep from asking him why he didn't just use Cutter's gun, partly because every inch of his tone implied that now was no time to argue, but mostly because he'd taken a literal bullet for her. She handed him back his gun. He took it. "Now, come on. Let's go."

She ran, dodging between the trees with Jacob right behind her, expecting at any moment to hear gunfire behind them. The trees parted and a long open slab of rock spread out in front of her, making a smooth gray platform. She stopped short, her feet on the edge of the tree line. Once she ran out, there'd be no cover.

The roar of rushing water ahead mingled with the thrum of the helicopter above.

"Go!" Jacob shouted. "Trust me!"

A rope ladder tumbled down from the sky, dangling out over the stone ahead, promising rescue and survival. She gasped for breath and ran for it, feeling her footsteps slip as they crossed the smooth wet rock. She leaped for the ladder, gripped it tightly and started climbing, rung after rung, as it shook and swayed beneath her, tossing her like laundry in the wind.

For a moment, she thought she was going to fall. Then she felt the rope ladder go tight like she'd suddenly been anchored. She looked down. It was Jacob. He'd holstered his weapon and was awkwardly clinging to the rope one-handed below her. The helicopter rose, sending the ladder flying out over the raging water below. She glanced past Jacob to the river churning beneath them. Her stomach lurched. This was reckless. She couldn't do this.

"Grace!" Jacob shouted. "Look at me!"

She clenched her jaw and shifted her gaze to the strong and determined face of the man beneath her. His eyes met hers, a reassuring smile crossed his face and she felt something like a light switch on inside her.

"You're okay!" he shouted. "Just keep climbing!"

A spray of bullets ripped through the forest beneath them. The helicopter lurched upward, nearly throwing her into the trees. Jacob shouted in pain. Then as she watched, he fell backward through the air, tumbling down toward the river below. A scream ripped from her lungs. *No!* His body hit the water and went under. Her heart pounded. He couldn't be dead. He just couldn't be. The helicopter rose higher. Jacob's body surfaced. *Thank You, Lord!* The spontaneous prayer surged through her heart, She watched for a moment as he swirled in the water, fighting one-handed against the current and struggling to shed the weight of his bulletproof vest.

Jacob had taken a bullet for her and now he was going to drown.

She glanced to the sky and the safety of the helicopter above. Suddenly the memory of being fourteen-years-old and watching her father run from the police filled her mind. No, she wasn't like him. She didn't run, not from someone who needed her, not to save herself, no matter what. Well, now was as good a time to try praying as any.

God, if You're listening, help me save him. And get us both out of this forest alive.

She let go of the rope ladder and let her body fall toward the river.

FOUR

For a moment, there was nothing but a rush of air beating against her body and a sick feeling in the pit of her stomach as she plummeted through the air.

Help me! Please!

Her body hit the water with such a force and impact that, for a split second, she thought she'd missed the river and hit the shore. She was sucked under and the swirling rapids closed around her. Pain filled her limbs. Panic filled her chest. The water was so cold it seemed to cut through her, freezing the blood inside her veins. She forced her body back up toward the surface and gasped a breath of muggy air.

"Jacob!" she tried to scream, pushing her voice over the water's roar. "Jacob! Can you hear me?"

But she could barely hear her own voice before water swept over her again, overwhelming her lungs. She coughed hard, fighting to breathe. The smell and taste of the river overwhelmed her senses. Water rose in dark gray-and-white-capped walls around her. She wasn't swimming as much as fighting the current just to survive.

She was going to drown. She was going to die. And all to save some man she barely knew. What had she been thinking? Why had she done this to herself? She gasped a breath. No, she knew him. Maybe they weren't friends. But she knew he dedicated his life to saving victims and putting criminals away. He was the man, who instead of running to save himself, had thrown himself in the way of danger for her.

All she was doing now was returning the favor.

The reason she'd let go of that rescue ladder and let herself fall hit her like a defibrillator jolt to the heart. Yeah, she'd had no idea it would be like this, how hard the fall would hit her or how violently the water would beat and batter her. But even if she had, it wouldn't have stopped her. Because if it was like this for her, how much worse must it be for him?

She steeled herself and forced a deep breath into her core. For a moment, she swirled and scanned the river ahead. Then she saw an outcropping rock and brush jutting out into the river ahead of her, no more than a couple of feet wide. She swam for it. Her legs bashed against sharp stones submerged beneath the surface, her feet dug deep into the mud, her body draped over the tiny island and she clung there, letting fresh air fill her lungs as water rushed past her.

Now, come on, Gracey. What were you thinking, jumping off a helicopter ladder like that? A warm voice filled her mind that sounded like her mother. *What did I tell you about never leaping into trouble for some man?*

Grace laughed, even trying to imagine how she'd explain this to Mom and Frank when she made it back to Toronto. She could honestly say it made no difference that Detective Jacob was tall, handsome and not too shabby to look at. She'd have leaped to save him no matter what he looked like. Just as she knew he'd have done the same for her.

Thank You, God, that I made it this far. Now what?

She wasn't exactly sure why she'd decided to try praying again. She'd given up on God long before her father had been carted off the jail because of how women at church gossiped about the fact that she'd been born before Frank and Mom got married. She'd been bullied for years by a couple of peers in her youth group and felt pushed to the outside of the social circle because of the circumstances surrounding her birth. At first, she'd tried rebelling, breaking every rule she could think of to spite the God she hadn't even thought she believed in. But then after her father went to jail, she changed course and decided she'd be better. She'd work harder, achieve more, keep more rules and win more awards than every single girl whose judgmental mother had thought she wasn't good enough to be her daughter's friend.

But now she was scared, overwhelmed and really needed help.

Rock walls towered on both sides, lined with trees. Even if she could make it to shore, there was no way she could climb up there. Her only option was to swim down river, find a place she could make it to shore and then run down the bank, hoping to find him.

"Grace!" A voice filled the air—strong, and male, and utterly incongruous. "Hang on! I'm coming for you!"

"Jacob?" she called.

"Yes! Grace! Oh, thank You, God!" His prayer floated

toward her over the water, so filled with relief she thought this wasn't the first time since she'd dropped that he'd tried calling her name.

"Where are you?" she shouted. And wherever he was, did he really think he was in any position to rescue her? "Are you okay?"

"I'm fine. I'm just hanging onto a tree. You still in the water?"

"Yeah! Hanging onto a rock!"

"Keep hanging on! I'm going to figure out a way to come to you!"

Really? "How?"

"I don't know yet!" His voice came back to her. "But I promise you, I'll figure it out."

That she didn't doubt. Another laugh slipped through her lips. Not because his statement was funny. But because there was something oddly wonderful about the sheer determination in his voice. And somehow she knew that if she needed him, truly needed him, he'd probably drown trying to swim upriver with a shot arm before he gave up attempting to rescue her.

"How big is that tree?" she called.

"Pretty big," he shouted back. "It's split at the trunk but still anchored to the shore."

"Big enough to support two people's weight?" she asked.

"Yeah…"

"You hold on! I'm coming to you!"

"What?" he shouted. "Don't!"

But she'd already let go. Immediately the water seized hold of her again, tossing and turning her around as it carried her away.

She swam downriver. Her energy was revived. This time she was prepared and her limbs were strong from years of swimming at Toronto's Cherry Beach before work and canoeing alone in Ontario forests. Her determination was even stronger.

Then she saw him, sooner than she'd expected, just a few breaststrokes and a single turn of the river away from where she'd stopped. He was clinging with one arm to a long and thick pine tree that lay across the water like a bridge, anchored to the shore by a bent and split stump. About six feet of sheer rock face lay between the broken stump and the top of the ridge.

All right, she just had to hit the tree, make her way along it to the shore, then climb up. Easy.

"Inbound!" she shouted.

He turned and almost tried to reach for her, stretching out his one good hand as he leaned over the tree for support. She shook her head and steered out of his way. Her body hit the tree a few feet away from him, in between him and the shore. The tree shook under her weight. She grabbed on with both hands and turned toward him.

"Hey." She gasped for breath. "So what's the plan?"

Green eyes opened wide in a rugged face that was ashen pale. "Are you okay?" His voice was deeper and huskier than she remembered. "I saw you fall."

"I'm fine," she said. "But what about you? You fell—"

"It's nothing." He frowned. "A bullet pinged my boot. I momentarily lost my footing and my grip failed me. But it's really not a big deal—"

"You were shot! And fell into a river—"

"And I'm fine." His tone hardened. "Like I said, it's no big deal."

Did he think he was indestructible? Talking to him felt like they were two rivers battling to flow in opposite directions. "You're clearly not fine," she said. "You were—"

"Shot," he finished for her. "Yes, I know. But it's a flesh wound and I'm mostly fine. Why did you fall?"

"I didn't fall—"

"I saw you—"

"I let go on purpose."

He blinked. He stared at her, and his lips parted like he didn't know what to say.

"I let go of the ladder on purpose," she said again. "Because I saw you fall…"

Her voice trailed off. Why? Why was he looking at her like that?

"And so, you let go."

There was a question moving beneath his words that she couldn't quite decipher. "Well, yeah, you'd just taken a bullet for me. And I really didn't want you to drown. So I let go and dropped into the water to help you. Then the helicopter left."

Jacob's mouth closed slowly, and for the first time that she could remember, the great Jacob Henry seemed speechless and not by choice. For a second, he didn't say anything, neither did she, and instead they just clung there, side by side, gasping for breath as the water beat against them. And somehow she found it impossible to look away from his gaze. He was like no one she'd ever met before—ridiculously good-looking, impeccably professional, impossibly stubborn and all together infuriating. Back in the real world, there'd always been this weird and awkward tension that seemed to radiate off him, or maybe off both of them, whenever they came within a few feet of each other. Even suspended on a tree in a raging river, that tension hadn't dissipated at all. If anything, it was as strong as it had always been. An unexpected laugh slipped her lips before she could bite it back.

His eyebrows rose. "What?"

She shook her head for a second and debated telling him the truth. Then again, if she couldn't be honest with someone when she was suspended on a broken tree over a river with them after dropping from a helicopter, then when could she? "It's just that I've been fighting for just five minutes of your time for months and now we're stuck together."

His gaze drifted up to the sky and she wasn't sure if he was praying, searching for the long-gone helicopter or very slowly rolling his eyes. Possibly all three. The tree creaked beneath them and she wondered for the first time how it was managing to stay rooted with the weight of two people dragging it down.

"We need to get to shore," he said finally. "Do you think you'll be able to slide your way along to the rock and climb up?"

"Yeah," she said. "Can you?"

To her surprise, he smiled, very slightly, like he wasn't used to anyone talking to him like that. But all he said was, "Yeah, you go first. I'll follow. As long as we stay close, our combined weight should stabilize the tree and keep it from moving too much."

Okay then. She slid along the fallen trunk slowly,

moving hand over hand along the slippery bark and kicking her legs to fight against the current as it threatened to yank her down.

"Don't worry," Jacob said. "Don't overthink it. Just keep moving. I'm right behind you."

He clearly didn't know just how much overthinking was her strong suit. But somehow something about the simple sound of his voice encouraging her helped her block out the pain in her limbs and the relentless pull of the water. She gritted her teeth and focused on the rock. The tree rose higher and, for a moment, she felt her legs leave the water. But then she felt the comforting and stabilizing weight of Jacob beside her, rooting the tree beneath them and helping her regain her balance. She reached the rock wall and looked up. The sun had almost set and the steep granite gleamed in the muggy air. It was slippery, it was steep, and her arms and legs were already aching so hard she couldn't even imagine how she was going to make it up.

"It's okay." Jacob's voice was comforting, solid and strong. "You got this. You're going to hoist yourself up onto the tree, climb up the rock and be just fine. I've got total faith in you."

He did—she wasn't sure why he did. She believed him and what's more, she knew he was right, in a deep core way that completely bypassed her logical brain. The ever-pressing need to ask why niggled at the edges of her brain, but for once she pushed it away and told it to wait until she was back on dry land.

"You got this," Jacob said again, and she suddenly remembered he was the big brother of at least one other sibling, who also happened to be a detective.

"I know," she agreed. Was this what having an older brother was like? "Just haul myself out of the water onto the log, climb up the rock and I'm home free." Or at least back on dry land and out of the water.

She took the deepest breath she could and pushed her body up out of the water, grasping onto the splintered stump. Her legs swung into the air. Her arms screamed in pain from the pressure of supporting her weight. Then she half slithered and half crawled her way onto the stump.

"Good job!"

"Thanks." She didn't look back and fought the urge to tell him she didn't need a cheerleader. It's not like his encouragement was hurting any. Slowly she climbed on top of the fallen tree, digging her feet in beneath her as best she could and started climbing up the rock face, grasping onto jutting rocks and handfuls of scrub, until finally she felt the top. She slid onto the forest floor, gasped a breath—*Thank You, God!*—and prayed without even thinking.

"You okay?" Jacob's voice came from beneath her.

"Yeah." She sat up, slid to the ledge of the rock face and looked down. Jacob had already half hauled his body out of the water and was now draped over the edge of the tree, looking up at her. "How about you? How are you going to climb up that with one hand?"

His eyes scanned the slippery rock face. "I'll figure it out."

She twisted her lips in thought and looked around her. There was a thin but strong looking tree by the edge she could've anchored a rope to, if she'd had one. Her belt was leather and pretty sturdy but not long enough to lower down. Her backpack was all the way back upriver tucked inside her grounded canoe, near where she'd first been grabbed by Cutter. She could hear Jacob below her, struggling and grunting as he tried to climb up.

"Hang on," she called. "I'm just going to try to find a way to help you up."

"I'm okay," he shouted back.

She shook her head. "No, you're not. Just give me—"

Then she heard the crack of wood, loud and deafening, Jacob shouting and then a splash.

Pain seared through Jacob's shoulder as the full weight of his body fell into the grip of one hand. The loss of footing had been sudden, as the tree beneath him finally split free from the rock face and tumbled into the water. Now his feet scrambled in vein for any foothold on the slippery stone where the tree had once been. His fingers screamed in pain as his grip threatened to falter. Time ticked past in agonizing seconds.

"Grab my hand!" Grace's voice above him was strong and sharp as a command.

He glanced up. Grace was hanging over the ledge. Her hands reached out toward him.

"I'll pull you over!" he shouted.

"I'm fine!" she shouted back. "I'm anchored to a tree. Just do it!"

But how big was the tree? How well was she anchored? How much weight could it hold? There was no way she could be strong enough to support him. If he gave in and grabbed her hand, who's to say he wasn't going to yank her over and then they'd both drown? It was bad enough she thought she had to leap from a helicopter for whatever misguided reason.

The pain in his fingers grew. She lowered herself over farther until he felt her hand brush his.

Help me, Lord! What am I going to do?

"Jacob, come on!" she shouted. "I need your help to get out of here alive. If you let yourself drown, then what happens to me?"

She grabbed his hand and held it firm. He let go of the rock and clenched her hand. For a moment, he thought they were going to slip from each other's grasp. But then she latched her second hand around his as well, holding his hand in both of hers.

"You won't be able to lift me!"

"Then use my arm like a rope and climb up," she grunted. Her breaths were shallow, and he had no doubt her arms and back were in agony. "Your legs still work, right?"

He laughed, not that he meant to, but because she was utterly infuriating, and not entirely in a bad way. White-capped water churned beneath him. He swung his legs up and planted them against the rock, hearing her almost yelp in pain at the sudden shift in weight. But all she said was, "Don't let go!"

He suspected she had no idea how extraordinary she was.

In six long painful steps, he was up. She helped haul him over the ledge. He crawled over, let go of her hands and then collapsed on his back. He stared up at the sky, wishing beyond any reasonable hope for the sight and sound of Kevin's helicopter. Instead, dark clouds filled his gaze. Wind shook the trees around him. Pain radiated through his body and shot through his shoulder, mingled with overwhelming gratitude to be back on dry land. Grace collapsed beside him and they lay there, side by side on their backs, panting and gasping on the muddy ground. Her arm brushed against his unwounded one and rested there. Somehow the slight touch reminded him of what it was like to be sitting beside a girl as a teenager, so close their shoulders touched, and trying to get up the courage to hold her hand. Not that dating had ever been a serious possibility after Faith had been killed. Grief had collapsed on top of his family, threatening to destroy them all under its weight. His parents and brothers had needed him to help keep them all together. So he'd quit hockey and soccer to be home more after school. He'd taken on a weekend job at the local supermarket to help with the household bills. Even as, in the past two years, he'd watched first Trent, then Max and finally Nick find strong, beautiful and amazing women to spend the rest of their lives with, he'd never felt the longing for a partner to share the load, join his life or even hold his hand. Not until now. And he didn't know what to make of it. He didn't take her hand. He didn't even let his fingers brush against hers. And yet he didn't move his arm away. Neither did she.

"Are you hurt?" he asked the moment he found his voice.

"Cold, wet and a bit banged up," she said. "But I'm okay. How are you?"

Cold, wet, in pain, frustrated, worried and confused was the response that crossed his mind. But the words that left his mouth were, "You shouldn't have let go of that helicopter ladder."

"That's a funny way to say *thank you for saving my life*." She sat up.

His spine stiffened, pushing him to a seating position. Yes, she'd helped him. But claiming she'd saved him was taking it a step too far. His teeth clenched. "There was no reason for you to put your life in danger like that."

"You would have drowned!"

"I would've found a way!"

Who was this woman? She had no idea who he was, what he'd lived through or what he was capable of. She had no idea what it meant to be a Henry and she never would. Even if she hadn't been a reporter, Grace Finch was the last person he'd ever confide in about Faith's death, what it had done to him, just how long and hard he'd searched for the truth, and how close he'd finally come to finding out who her killer was.

"Right," Grace said, as if responding to something he hadn't even said. Her wet olive green canvas jacket seemed to be plastered on in uneven folds, reminding him of his creative mother's textured art. "Because sheer willpower and determination are enough to keep a person from drowning."

"Sheer willpower and determination are enough for a lot of things!" he shot back. A flash of something hot moved through his veins, like a sudden fire he'd never felt before exploding out of nowhere. What was it about this woman? Nothing ever got under his skin like she did. She must've seen it too, because her dark eyes widened.

"Well, Detective Henry, that's actually something we can both agree on," she said. Then she shrugged like she was tossing his words off her shoulders. "Besides, like I said, you took a bullet for me. Figure this makes us even."

She leaned forward, and it was only then he realized she'd looped her belt around her ankle and fastened it to a thin pine tree. That was all there'd been to keep them both from drowning? Just how gutsy was she? Slowly she unfastened her leg from the trunk.

"I also have a first aid kit," she added. "Along with some food and camping supplies in my bag. Do you want me to check the bullet wound in your arm now? Or wait to see if we can reach my bag first?"

He noticed not checking his wound hadn't been included as an option.

"Thankfully it's just a graze. The bullet isn't in the wound, and if anything it's a lot cleaner than it was." He laughed to show he was trying to make a joke. Her lips turned in an equally practiced smile to show she was acknowledging that, and he immediately regretted not being more authentic and real. "Honestly, I'm worried that with how muddy we both are right now we'd just contaminate it and I don't want to risk getting an infection. Beyond that, I'm a bit dizzy but I'm not worried about blood loss, especially as the bleeding seems to have stopped. Where is your bag?"

"Back where Cutter caught up with me," she said. "It's in my canoe, which I had pulled up onto the shore. I'd taken it off to see about setting up camp and he spotted me before I could go back for it. Hopefully it's still there. I've lost my Taser. Tell me you still have the guns."

Heat rose to his face. That should've been the first

thing he'd checked once crawling to shore, instead of lying there with a brain full of ridiculous thoughts while his lungs fought to catch his breath. He did a quick spot check. Cutter's gun was in his ankle holster and his own was at his waist. Then he reached for his right breast pocket and worry stabbed like a spear through his core. He'd lost his phone when he'd shed the bulletproof vest. The wind whipped harder. Thunder rumbled above, ominous and unhelpful. He felt his face pale. "Guns, yes, but I've lost my phone. Please tell me you've a phone."

"In my bag," she said. "But the signal was really faint and kept cutting out."

He wasn't surprised. Getting a phone signal this deep in these woods was unreliable in the best of times and when the storm hit, reaching the outside world would be all but impossible. Her dark eyes searched his face and he watched as worry pooled in their depths. "What's wrong?"

"I have no way to contact the helicopter," he said. "There's a bad storm coming and it might be hours before they can launch another aerial search. They'll probably send both RCMP officers and Search and Rescue to our location, but that could take hours. Until then, we're stranded."

FIVE

"*Stranded?*" Grace felt her own voice break as she said the word. What did he mean? Her chest tightened and for a moment she felt her own heart beating so hard it hurt to breathe. No, she'd already spent too many hours in these woods. She wasn't about to get stuck here any longer. As if on cue, the sky broke and the rain hit harder, pouring down around them like a sheet of tiny pebbles, marring her vision and pounding against her skin.

Jacob pulled himself to standing, using his good arm for support. "Kevin can't fly in this weather. He'll have to wait until the wind dies down and the skies clear. It's supposed to be a very bad storm. They're talking major flooding."

Okay, so canoeing back to her car was out of the question and it had taken her six hours to get this deep into the woods when she had been able to travel through the network of rivers, with a combination of paddling and portaging. When she'd mapped it on the GPS, the hike alone would've been closer to twelve hours. Not to mention they now knew there were at least two armed killers in the woods.

But it's not like they had other better options. She scrambled to her feet. "We can hike back to my car."

"You want to hike all night in this weather?" he asked, but it wasn't really a question. "I can barely see in this rain. We need to hold tight and hole up somewhere until the rain clears and help can get to us. But we'll start with finding your phone. Hopefully it'll be possible to get a signal to the outside world."

The fist of fear in her chest grew tighter. She wasn't sure how successful she was at hiding it, because when he noticed her expression, he added, "Trust me, I like this as little as you do."

Really? At least he was armed.

"The good news is that I saw a cabin not far from where I rappelled down to find you," he said. "Fortunately, compasses are waterproof and if we backtrack, I should be able to find it."

A cabin? *Her cabin?* Did Jacob actually know the location of the cabin where her father apparently had left proof of his innocence? Was Jacob actually going to lead her there?

"Obviously I'll have to scout it out and make sure none of the convicts made it there first," Jacob went on. He started walking. She followed. "Yeah, it'll be a risk, but it's a risk I'm willing to take to get us out of the storm. I don't want us getting struck by lightning or hit by a falling tree. Not to mention the rivers are going to rise. At least in the cabin we can dry off. And you can get some rest. Sleeping will be out of the question for me. I'll stay up all night, guard the door and make sure you're safe."

They kept walking. Her mind spun as her body

pushed through the rain, the trees and the thick, slippery mud. What if her father was there, waiting for her? What if he'd left something for her and Jacob found it?

What if Jacob discovered that she was the daughter of a man he despised?

And yet what else could she do? They were in the woods, the rain was relentless, night was falling and whether she liked it or not, Jacob was her best hope for surviving if Cutter and Driver found her.

"We can take turns keeping watch," she said. "You need rest even more than I do."

He didn't argue but he didn't respond either, leaving her to guess if he'd heard her. They kept walking, climbing over logs and pushing through branches. The rain poured down around them, hard and heavy, striking with a ferocity that made it impossible to do anything but slowly and painstakingly keep moving forward. Jacob's eyes scanned the woods as they walked. His posture was almost relaxed and yet there was also an alertness to him, something about the way he walked that implied he was ready for danger at any moment. It was comforting, but not surprising. For all the times he'd walked past her at crime scenes, without so much as making eye contact, she'd seen more than enough of the detective to notice the unusual way he carried himself. There was a casualness to him, a saunter, a way he entered a space with his tall broad-shouldered form that projected the idea that there was nothing to worry about and everything was going to be okay. It never seemed fake either, unlike other cops, like detective Warren Scott whose charm turned on and off like a faucet. She didn't know how to put it, only that it projected reassurance, confidence and authority without being tense, aggressive or stressful. She liked it.

Suddenly he stopped, turned and looked back at her through the wall of rain beating down between them, like he'd known she'd been studying him and wasn't sure he liked it. She felt his eyes searching her face in the dying light, as if there was something written beneath the surface of her skin he was looking for. If so, he wasn't going to find it. For a very long moment, he didn't say anything. Neither did she. He wouldn't be the first person she'd known to use long silences to get the other person to speak first. But if so, he'd met his match there. He rolled his shoulders back, his spine straightened and there was something about the gesture that reminded her of a mythological creature unfurling his wings. Yeah, she'd seen him do that move before too. To her embarrassment, a laugh slipped her lips before she could catch it. His eyebrows rose.

"Can I ask what's so funny?" he asked.

"You have this thing you do with your posture," she said, raising her voice to be heard over the storm. "In reality you must be what, six foot two or six foot three? But you have this way of walking that makes you look the same height as all the cops that are barely six feet tall. Like you don't want to intimidate them or something."

Even through the rain, she could hear the curious half-smile in his voice. "Oh, really?"

"Really," she said. "But then you kind of unfurl to your full height sometimes. When you want to, I don't know, be taken seriously or project an air of authority? To be honest, I haven't quite pinpointed why you do it. Are you aware you're doing it? Is it something you used to do as a kid? You're the oldest sibling in your family, right?"

He paused for a moment, standing there in the rain, and she thought he was about to answer. Then he started walking again. "No, we're not doing this. Let me make one thing clear, this is a rescue mission, not an interview."

"Okay, fair enough." Her footsteps quickened. Her hand brushed his arm. "You're the one who suddenly stopped. Clearly you had something on your mind."

He kept walking. "Yes, and then you reminded me that I'm talking to a reporter."

"What's that supposed to mean?"

Still, he didn't stop. "I mean, that I've been processing and thinking a lot while we've been walking and I've realized I don't like being lied to."

"Does anyone like being lied to?" she asked.

Now that made his footsteps falter and she thought for a moment he was about to stop, but he didn't.

"I'm not accusing you of anything," he said. "I'm just trying to figure out what kind of person I'm stranded in the woods with. And I think it's very unlikely an award-winning crime reporter just happens to be in the middle of nowhere the same day three convicted criminals escaped from a prison van. How do you account for that stunning coincidence?"

"Why are you quizzing me now?" she shot back. What exactly had he been *processing* while they walked? "I thought you said this wasn't an interview."

His feet froze. He spun around so suddenly she nearly walked into him.

"Let me make one thing clear," he said. "You are not going to interview me in the woods or use the fact we're stranded out here to question me about anything. You may be a reporter back in the real world, but right now, you're just a civilian who I'm rescuing. I, however, am still a cop—I will always be a cop—and I'm still on duty, so I expect you to tell me everything and anything you know about the three men who escaped prison and how you just happen to be here in the middle of it—"

"And I have a constitutional right not to answer police questions according to the Canadian Charter of Rights and Freedoms." She felt her voice rise. No, he wasn't going to play a badge on her. She knew far too much about police procedures, starting at far too young an age. "Do you want my full name and address for the record, Officer? That much you have the right to ask and I'll give it. But beyond that, I give you my word that I knew absolutely nothing about the prison escape before Cutter jumped me. Believe me, I'm not stupid enough to go running out into the middle of nowhere, six hours canoeing and portaging from my car without a decent weapon, or a cell signal, or any kind of backup if I'd known there was a killer loose in the woods, let alone two."

"Three," he said. "Two that we know of, possibly three. You're forgetting that Hal Turner, dirty cop and cop killer, could be out here too for all we know."

Oh, no, she definitely had not forgotten about him.

"And I'm not trying to start a fight," Jacob added.

Maybe not. But offence was one of the best defenses she had.

"What do you think my angle is here, Detective?"

she asked. "Do you think I'm actually stupid enough to run out here to interview a killer or three, in the middle of nowhere, in a storm?"

"Don't put words in my mouth, please," he said. He turned and kept walking. "That's not what I'm saying, and I told you I'm not trying to start a fight. But if my sense of direction is right, we're almost back to where you left your stuff and about ten minutes away from the cabin. And before I risk my life to go in to the cabin to sweep it for criminals, I want to make sure I know the person whose back I'm protecting. And for this whole walk, there's been one thought I haven't been able to get out of my head."

She felt her chin rise. "Which is?"

"Which is," he said, "there's something you're not telling me, Grace. Have no doubt, I will figure it out. And until I know what it is, I'm not going to trust you."

He kept walking. He could hear her spluttering behind him, but he didn't turn around. He'd been wanting to say that for a while, and he could tell by the trees and rocks around them that they'd already passed the place where Cutter had shot at him. They reached a low patch of ground by the water's edge and he kept watch while she got her bag and checked the contents. Good news was nothing was missing. Bad news was her phone didn't have a signal and the battery was close to dead. They pulled her canoe higher into the forest, away from the water and then tied both ends to trees to keep it grounded in case the river rose. Then they kept walking, using his compass and memory of the natural landscape to find the cabin.

The whole time they'd been trudging through the forest he'd sensed Grace behind him, almost like a physical itch he hadn't been able to scratch or a musical note he hadn't been able to tune out. No, more like a magnet. An invisible magnet that had always been there, which simultaneously pulled him in and pushed him back again, every single time he'd seen her face in a crowd or her name pop up on his phone or computer screen.

The trees cleared and then he could see the cabin. It was a more of a run-down shack really, made of brick, with one small window set high in the wall and a sloping roof that provided some shelter over a single step at the front door. The door swung open on its hinges, back and forth, creaking open, then slamming shut as it was pulled and pushed, opened and closed by the wind. He stopped and held up his good hand toward her, motioning her to stop. Silence fell as she stopped moving behind him. But he didn't turn around. Instead, he sensed her there, as if Grace were some kind of phantom limb he hadn't known he'd lost.

"Stay behind me," he said. "If I raise my hand, stay back until I wave you forward. If anything goes haywire, get yourself to safety and stay hidden until I find you. Worst-case scenario, rescue helicopters have infrared cameras. Someone will find you."

"Got it." The strength and timbre in her voice made him turn. Courage filled the eyes that returned his gaze, the kind he'd only ever seen in the face of someone who knew fear all too well. Alongside it ran another emotion, one which almost shocked him, considering the argument they'd been having moments earlier: trust.

"You sure you're okay?" she asked.

There was a depth to her worry that somehow disarmed him. It wasn't pitying or arrogant; it was compassionate, and suddenly he could imagine how she really was the kind of woman who'd drop from a helicopter to save someone from drowning. Truth was, he wasn't okay. Not even close. At least not in the deeper beneath-the-surface way that she was asking. For a moment, he was tempted to tell her just that. He was tempted to tell her about the relentless pain in his arm and that he had to concentrate to keep his limbs from shaking. He wanted to admit he was worried, because while he was still a pretty good shot with his left hand, it was nothing compared to what he could do with his right. He wanted to tell her that the idea of having to protect her, against escaped convicts and a deadly storm, almost scared him, because for some reason something about the idea of letting her down shook him to the core. Then maybe, after saying all that, he wanted to confess how much he hated the fact that he didn't trust her. Because he wanted to trust her. He wanted to rely on her. He wanted them to have each other's backs and know they were in this together. But he didn't, he couldn't, because he was the cop and she was the civilian. She was his responsibility, not his friend, let alone his partner. This was a rescue mission, nothing more.

"Please don't worry about me," he said. "Just stay close and follow my lead. Okay?"

She nodded. "Got it."

He allowed himself one long, lingering look at her face, even though he was barely able to make out her features between the darkness and the rain, wondering why, out of all of the faces he'd seen in his life, this one was so hard to look away from. Then he turned around, whispered a prayer and started across the clearing, feeling the rain batter his skin and watching the door swing open and shut ahead of him. He reached the cabin, his knee caught the door and he froze as he waited for his eyes to adjust to the gloom. The cabin's main room was plain and rectangular, with thick log walls and wooden plank floors. A simple wooden table and two chairs sat by the far wall, while the near wall had a counter and sink with a bucket underneath where the plumbing would've gone. A single window sat high in the wall above his head, and two doors lay to his right. He glanced back and saw Grace standing exactly where he'd left her. He waved her forward, and she crossed the clearing quickly and smoothly. They crowded together under the doorway, out of the rain in the small dry patch caused from the overhanging roof. He leaned in toward her and the scent of her filled his senses, reminding him of warmth, wildflowers and home.

"So far, so good," he said. "I'm going to go check out the bedrooms."

She nodded and reached for her bag. "You want my flashlight?"

"No, you hold onto it." He said. "I have a small light I can clip on my shoulder." If he'd had both hands available, he'd have held a big flashlight in one and his service weapon in the other. But he wasn't about to put a civilian's life at risk by getting her to walk beside him with a flashlight. "Just stay here, right inside the door and out of sight."

She exhaled, just sharp enough for him to wonder if

she'd meant anything by it, but all she said was, "Okay, got it."

"Back in a second." He crossed the empty room, keeping his weapon at the ready. Boards creaked underneath his feet. The smell of cobwebs and dust filled the air. His boots left small puddles on the floor. He pushed the closest door open and paused. It was a bedroom, as thin and narrow as a cupboard, with a bare and single cot suspended by two chains from the wall.

The wind howled outside, high-pitched and angry, followed by a crash of thunder. He steeled a breath. Like Noah's ark, this tiny cabin had survived countless storms in the eightysome years since it'd been built. It would get them safely through tonight. He turned and stepped backward into the main room and glanced back at where Grace stood, her body a dark silhouette by the door. "All clear. Just one more room to go."

He stepped into the second bedroom. This room was barely any wider, with a tiny skylight in the slanted ceiling and two thin cots on opposite walls, and oddly the very small bedroom he'd shared with his brother Trent back at the Henry family farmhouse filled his mind. He stepped inside. Something was suspended from the skylight, tossing and spinning on a thin chain, seemingly caught in a gust of wind, whipping in through a crack in the window frame. Something left by a camper long ago? He stepped deeper into the room.

"Hey, Jacob?" Grace called. "Can we close the front door now? The wind and rain are really picking up."

"Just give me a second." He walked toward the skylight, his eyes struggling to make out the shape as it spun and danced in front of him. A thin layer of dust covered every other surface in the cabin, but the item was so shiny it could've just been polished. The floor creaked beneath him. He holstered his weapon, reached up and grabbed the pendant, hearing the tack that had been suspending it fall off and clatter to the ground. Cool metal brushed against his fingertips. It was a heart-shaped locket, about an inch high and an inch wide, and so achingly familiar it suddenly hurt to breathe.

He'd seen a locket exactly like this before. He'd saved up, he'd bought it, he'd had his family's name engraved on it and then he'd given it to Faith for Christmas. Then just a few months later, she'd been wearing it the day she was strangled at the side of the road.

Police hadn't found it with the body.

He ran his fingers over the locket, feeling the rough engraving of a word beneath his thumb. His heart beat like an invisible hand had reached into his chest and grabbed hold of it, and it was struggling to escape.

No, it couldn't be. It just couldn't.

"Hey, Jacob?" Grace called.

He held it up toward his flashlight. Bright light shone on the small gold locket in his hand, illuminating a single word that seared like fire through his mind.

Henry.

No, no, it couldn't be his sister's locket. He was exhausted, he'd lost a lot of blood, his mind must be playing tricks on him.

Something moved behind him in the darkness, rising like a coiled snake from the corner of the room. He spun back. There was a man behind him, a featureless shadow in dark clothes and a ski mask. Jacob reached for his weapon. But before his hand had even brushed the butt, the man grabbed him by the arm, clamping his hand over Jacob's bullet wound. Blinding pain filled Jacob's mind so suddenly he nearly blacked out. The man pushed him backward. Jacob's body hit the floor. The locket fell from his hand.

Then he heard Grace scream his name.

SIX

Grace's own screams echoed in her ears as the figure barreled across the cabin toward her, leaving her no time to think, no time to process, no time to do anything but act. Her brain spun to grasp onto the details of what she was seeing. He was large and swamped in dark shapeless clothes with just the whites of his eyes showing through a full-face ski mask. His hand shot out as he ran toward her.

Her fingers tightened their grip on the long and hard metal shaft of her camping flashlight. She swung it around like a cudgel and hit nothing but empty air, as he barreled into her, shoving her so hard against the wall her head slammed into the wood. One hand grabbed her throat. The other pressed her shoulder back against the wall. The flashlight began to slip from her grasp. A gun loomed before her eyes as if he was struggling to remove the safety.

If he killed her, she'd die fighting. *Help me, God!* A prayer crossed her heart as she swung her hand up and hit him hard on the side of the head with the flashlight.

Her attacker stumbled back. Then gunfire sounded

beside her, splitting the air as the wood behind her exploded into splinters. She dropped to the floor and rolled. Had he misfired? Had he been trying to kill her? Either way, he wasn't going to get off another shot. She kicked him hard, collapsing his knee and sending him falling to the ground. The flashlight slipped from her hand and hit the ground, sending light spinning in circles as it slid across the floor.

"Grace!" Jacob's voice sounded from the other room. "Hold on! I'm coming!"

A second gunshot echoed in the darkness. Plaster rained down from the ceiling above her. A light flickered.

"Police!" Jacob shouted. She looked up toward the beam of light on Jacob's shoulder as he stumbled through the doorway. "Get down! Drop your weapon! Or I'll shoot!"

The figure bolted through the door and ran out into the night. In a moment, she'd lost sight of his form to the forest and the rain. She kicked the door closed and leaped to her feet to lock it.

"Don't!" Jacob shouted. "I'm going after him!"

"No, you're not!" Grace stepped in front of the door. "You're injured, and he's armed! Do you really think you'll be able to track him in this storm?"

But he didn't even look at her, as he reached past her for the door. "Out of the way. Now! I can't let him escape."

He pushed past her and ran out of the cabin.

"Jacob!" she yelled. "Stop! Come back!"

He kept going and, in a moment, she lost sight of even his flashlight in the storm. She grabbed onto the door frame. The rain fell in sheets smacking like a cascade of rocks hitting the ground.

"Jacob!" she yelled again. But heard nothing except the wind howling back in response. He was gone. He'd left her. She found herself remembering again what it had been like to be fourteen and left alone as her father bolted from the coffee shop. She picked the flashlight up off the floor.

She ran back to the door and for one long moment shone her flashlight beam out into the darkness like a beacon, praying for Jacob's form to appear. Then she gave up and slammed the door closed again. She felt for a lock and found two of them, one on the doorknob and a heavy-duty deadbolt on the door above. She locked both.

Then she swung her flashlight around the room.

"Okay, God, so as You know, there's a major storm and at least two killers outside," she prayed. Her voice was quivering but seemed to be growing stronger as she went. "Should I stay here and wait for Jacob, Lord? If I stay here, I'm a sitting duck. If I go out into the storm, I could get hit by lightning, or a falling tree, or drown if I stumble too close to a river. And if I stay here, Jacob can find me."

Was praying helping? She wasn't sure. But while her heart still pounded as hard as ever, she could also feel the steady calm of her journalistic instincts filling her mind. Logic and facts had always been her allies. She swung the flashlight around the cabin and focused on the details. There was a crater in the ceiling and another in the wall from where the masked man's bullets had struck, but neither one was completely through. Good to know both the walls and ceiling were reasonably thick. The room had only one window, but it was high up in the wall and had heavy-duty shutters. She leaped up onto the counter, thankful it supported her weight, reached for the shutters and bolted them closed. The room fell even darker. She climbed back down.

There. It would be fairly hard for someone to get through without a ladder, and the shutters would provide enough barrier against gunfire to give her time to get out of the line of fire. She started for the bedrooms. Each had a small skylight and while neither had shutters, both were locked from the inside and too small for a person to climb through.

She finished searching one bedroom and stepped into the other, shining the flashlight along the floor. Something golden glinted in its beam. She bent down and picked it up. It was a locket, gold and smooth, with a single word engraved on it: *Henry.*

Like Jacob Henry? Her fingers slid down the side. It popped open. Inside was a picture of a smiling family. Two parents, two boys and a girl crowded, hugging and smiling, into the frame. There was an infant in the mother's arms. Who was this?

Banging came so hard on the door that she could hear the hinges rattle. Her hand rose to her heart as she looped the locket chain around her wrist.

"Grace! It's me, Jacob. Let me in!"

Thank You, God!

"Coming!" She ran back through the main room of the cabin and yanked the locks back. Jacob tumbled through the doorway and collapsed onto the floor, soaking and exhausted like someone had sapped the remaining oxygen from his body. She closed the door and locked it behind him.

"Are you okay?" He gasped for breath. "Did he hurt you?"

"No." She dropped to her knees beside him. "I'm fine."

"I couldn't find him!" He looked up at her and pain filled his eyes that was so acute it seemed to rip his usual professional mask in two and let her look through to the real, vulnerable and hurting man inside. "I tried but I lost him."

"That's okay," she started. "At least you're safe…"

But her words froze on her tongue as his eyes darted from her face to the locket in her hands. Then something hardened behind his eyes. "Give that to me."

"I found it on the floor," she said. "It's a girl's locket. It says Henry. There's a family inside. Is it yours?"

"Yeah." He holstered his weapon and stretched out his hand. "It was my sister's."

He felt the locket fall into his hand and closed his fingers around it. "I need you to promise me that everything I tell you right now, in this cabin, is forever and permanently off the record and you won't repeat it to anyone ever. You are not about to interview me. Okay?"

"Of course! How can you ask me that? Jacob, you're not a source to me and I definitely don't feel like a reporter toward you…"

"Just promise me, please." To his chagrin, he heard his voice threaten to break. "Please, Grace. Before I tell you about the locket, I need to hear you say those words."

"This isn't an interview!" she said. "Everything you tell me is off the record. I promise that I am never going to repeat anything you tell me, ever, unless we both agree it's on the record. Trust me, I know how to keep secrets." Sincerity pushed through her voice. Worry filled her eyes. Her now-empty hand reached into the darkened space between them. "Please, Jacob. Tell me what's going on."

"Okay." He nodded. "Just give me a couple of minutes to first get my head around what I'm about to say. Because to be honest, I haven't figured out where to start. In the meantime, how about you get out that first aid kit and take a look at my arm?"

Thunder slammed the sky outside. The trees shook. And for a long moment, he thought she was going to argue.

"Okay." She set down her flashlight and picked up her bag. "The window shutters are bolted from the inside. I couldn't find shutters on the skylights in the bedroom, but I locked them and they're pretty small. Both the ceiling and wall seem to have done a pretty good job withstanding those bullets. Seemed whoever built the ranger log cabins in the 1930s built them to last."

There was a softness and something almost comforting or reassuring about the way she changed the topic. Like a sensitive interviewer. No, like a friend. He wasn't quite sure what to think of it or why she'd done it, but he was thankful nonetheless.

He had no idea how long he'd been out there, floundering in the storm, trying to find the man who'd attacked them in the cabin. But it had been useless. He couldn't see which way the man had gone and could barely see where he was going. He'd just been thrashing around, with only Grace's shouting to remind him where the cabin had been.

Then he'd dropped to his knees in the dirt and sobbed as if holding his little sister's locket in his hands had torn open a cut so deep inside him it would never be able to fully heal. *Why?* was all he'd been able to pray at first. *Why this? Why now? Why here?*

Why did my sister die?

Then he'd dragged himself to his feet and jogged back, with two thoughts filling his mind. One was that he'd been wrong to leave Grace. The other was that he couldn't keep what had happened secret from her, not with how he could feel the pain of his sister's death coursing through him like a fresh and bleeding wound. He could try not to talk about it. He could do his best to be nothing but an impersonal professional and maybe he'd succeed for the first hour or three. But thoughts of Faith and the locket would preoccupy him and block out his ability to concentrate on anything else. It would distract him from doing what needed to be done.

"Do you think we're safer staying here than going out in the storm?" she asked.

"I do." He nodded, thankful she'd said *safer* instead of *safe*. "Neither option is a good one. But at least in here, we'll be dry and free from getting struck by lightning or anything. It's not that far from where we fell, so when they send a rescue helicopter this will probably be one of the first areas they search. To my way of thinking, I'd rather defend a fort than get hunted in the woods."

He let her help him out of his long-sleeved shirt,

until he was sitting there in just a T-shirt. He glanced down at the ugly red bullet wound cutting across his arm and thanked God it wasn't worse. The gash was longer than he'd expected but seemed fairly shallow. "I don't think it's that bad."

She kneeled beside him and turned the flashlight toward him.

"I've seen worse," she said.

"Really?" he asked. "Where?"

"Crime scenes," she said. "Natural disasters." She got antiseptic wipes out of her kit and cleaned her hands thoroughly. "I did both first aid training and lifeguarding in high school and college. You'd be surprised how often, as a reporter, I reach a victim before police and paramedics do. My editor, Olivia Ash, always said that first we stop the bleeding, then we ask the questions. Though usually all someone needs is a hug, or a bottle of water, or help getting to the actual paramedics. Like Olivia said, we're always a human being first and a reporter second."

He'd met Olivia a couple of times, thanks to the fact that her sister, Chloe, was marrying his brother Trent in two days' time. He didn't know her well, but knew her enough to know that she had a kind heart and a dedication to reporting the truth. But Olivia wasn't like most journalists.

"I've seen you at dozens of crime scenes and I've heard you shout plenty of questions my direction and I've never seen you…" His voice trailed off as he suddenly realized there was no good way to end his sentence.

"You've never seen me what?" she asked. "You've never seen me help someone?"

Maybe not in those words, but close enough that he wasn't going to add insult to injury by denying it. "I'm sorry," he said. "I don't know what I was thinking."

"Well then maybe you just weren't paying close enough attention," she said.

She pulled a wad of cotton from the first aid kit and poured some alcohol on it. The sharp and clean smell filled the small space. Then he felt the stinging coolness of it against his wound. He wondered if he should apologize again. He'd been afraid this would happen. That his mood would be off. If he didn't open up, thoughts of what had happened to his sister would just eat away inside him.

Lord, I feel like there's no good way to start this. Please help me speak clearly. Help Grace listen. Just be here with us right now.

"When I was fourteen years old, someone murdered my little sister, Faith."

Grace sat back as if the words had landed in the room and sent invisible shockwaves rippling into the air and pushing her back.

"I'm sorry," she said softly. "That must've been really hard."

"It was. Thank you. If I'm honest, that's where my dislike of the press comes from. It's like they pulled away at the edges of our pain and made it worse."

"I'm sorry," she said again.

"Thank you," he repeated.

For a long moment, neither of them said anything. They just sat there, in the cabin, in the storm, with his eyes on her face and her eyes on his in the dim glow of the flashlight. Then she went back to cleaning his wound and he went back to his story.

"That's her in the middle of the picture in the locket," he said. "I'm the tall one on the left with the goofy grin. Then that's Trent next to me. The baby in my mother's arms is Max. My youngest brother, Nick, wasn't born yet. I gave Faith the locket for Christmas, about six months before she died."

He paused for a moment. Grace set the cotton down, pulled out a strip of gauze and started bandaging the gash with it.

"Someone tried to grab her off the road when she was walking home from school," he said, oddly thankful he was talking to a journalist. At least she'd be familiar with the idea of just focusing on facts. "Judging by the evidence, she was walking home alone, a car stopped, someone got out and tried to kidnap her. She fought back." He swallowed hard. "He strangled her and then left her there at the side of the road. A motorist found her and called the police. I was the one who opened the door when they came."

Grace gently took his other hand in hers and pressed it against the gauze on his arm. "Can you hold this here while I cut some adhesive tape?"

Their fingers lingered there together for a moment, touching and slightly linked. Then she pulled away and reached for the adhesive tape. He closed his eyes and listened to the rain pounding down around them and the wind shaking the walls. Oddly, the storm that had driven them indoors was now also a shield against any type of coordinated attack or ambush. Anyone who wanted to hurt them would have to fight through the wind and the rain to get to them, and it would make the cabin almost impossible to see in the darkness.

"A day hadn't even passed before the journalists showed up," he said, knowing it wasn't even close to the most important part of the story, but feeling like it was something he needed her to know. "We had reporters camped out in front of our house and following Trent and me to school. I won't even pretend that's not the reason why I don't like journalists. They're like carrion birds picking over the lives of others. That's why I reacted the way I did whenever you approached me, and why I ignored your emails. A big part of why, anyway."

He wasn't about to admit he was attracted to her. And wasn't quite sure why he'd needed her to know just how much he disliked journalists.

"It's not that I didn't respect you," he added quickly. "Truth be told, I think you might be one of the most interesting women I've ever met. You're smart and brave, and your articles are really well written."

"Thank you," she said. "I didn't realize you'd read anything I'd written. You're pretty interesting and brave yourself."

A bang sounded somewhere outside the cabin like a distant tree falling in the forest. Jacob stood up slowly, walked over to the door, opened it and looked out for a long moment. Grace set the tape and gauze slowly back in the first aid kit and closed it. The two plastic clasps clicked shut loudly.

"All clear?" she asked.

"Yeah." Jacob turned back. "I think the storm's taking down a lot of trees. We might be looking at a whole new landscape tomorrow."

He closed and locked the door again.

"What's said in this cabin doesn't leave this cabin," she said. "Right?"

"Yeah."

"You won't dig into my business, and I won't dig into yours. Agreed?"

"Of course." He sat back down beside her on the floor. "Unless you're about to confess to either committing or knowledge of a crime."

"My father was arrested when I was fourteen," she said. She pulled her knees up into her chest and wrapped her arms around them. "I hadn't seen him in a couple of years when suddenly he wanted to go get donuts. We're sitting there in Tims when the police were everywhere, shouting at him to get down. He ran out, they chased him." She shrugged. "But I never thought to hate the cops. When I read about his crimes in the media, I never thought to blame the press. I only blamed him. And God."

Finch. Grace Finch. The temptation to go searching through the crime database for her family name niggled at him. But as her eyes met his, he felt the weight of the promise he'd made in her gaze.

"Can I ask what he was arrested for?" he asked.

"No, you may not," she said. "I don't talk about my birth father or my background. I don't want my life to be judged by somebody else's mistakes. I just wanted you to know you weren't alone. I never had a sibling, let alone lost one. But I know what it's like to have your life torn apart."

Her hand stretched out into the darkness between them, her fingers brushed his arm, and something flickered in her eyes. It was like a desire to be seen, a desire to be known, and suddenly he had the feeling there was way more to her than he'd ever imagined.

"Maybe when I get to know you better, I might one day be willing to talk about my father," she said. And something in the timbre of her voice made him wonder if he was the first person she'd ever said that to. "Now, please tell me more about your sister."

"They never caught the person who killed her," he said. He leaned back into his elbow, reached into his pocket and slid her locket inside. "They never even found the car. They found a lot of DNA evidence under her fingernails, but it was never a match to anyone in the system. When I joined the force, I tried to look into it and discovered the remaining DNA sample had been destroyed. Maybe it was a clerical error. Maybe something went wrong. I don't know." He thought about the next part of the story and how vague he could keep it. "Please keep this between us, but a contact of mine said he recently uncovered something about misfiled police evidence boxes. There's a slim possibility he might be able to use that information to figure out what happened to her attacker's DNA sample. If I wasn't here with you, I'd be meeting him tonight."

"I'm sorry you're stuck here," she said.

"I'm not," he said, and for far more reasons than he'd ever be able to admit to her. "Because we can always reschedule the meeting and I just found this locket— Faith's locket—in the bedroom suspended from the skylight. Judging by the dust patterns, it hasn't been there long. Faith was wearing it the day she died. It was never recovered from her body." He watched as Grace's hand rose to her lips. "This means either Cutter, Driver or Turner had something to do with the death of my sister."

SEVEN

He watched as Grace leaped to her feet and started to pace.

"But that's not possible," she said. "It's just not. You've got to know that."

What was she talking about? What wasn't possible? He sat up straight. Of all the possible reactions, agitation hadn't been one he'd been expecting. "Yeah, I get how improbable it sounds. But I'm telling you that this is the locket my little sister was wearing the day she was murdered."

Grace stopped, turned and looked at him. For a long moment, she didn't say anything.

"But it's just not possible," Grace said, but softly and sadly, like she was talking to someone who wasn't even there. "If she died twenty-four years ago how could anyone possibly plant it here? If her killer took it with him and then he was arrested, how did he manage to smuggle it into prison with him and then smuggle it out again when he escaped today? They'd have taken all of his belongings from him when he was arrested—"

"I don't know!" He pushed up off the floor with his

good hand so hard he heard his palm smack against the wood. Now he started pacing too, until they were walking around each other in circles like they were both tigers trapped in a crate. "Maybe he hid it somewhere and retrieved it when he got out of prison. Maybe he did in fact smuggle it in and out of jail. Maybe he had an accomplice get it to him recently. Again, I don't know!" His voice rose, joining with the howl of the wind, crash of the thunder and the steady beat of the rain. "I'll admit it makes no sense. I'm confused, Grace. I'm beyond confused. I don't have a clue what's going on here or how my dead sister's locket got into a cabin in the middle of nowhere. Finding this locket was the most surreal, upsetting and unbelievable thing that's ever happened to me. And there's absolutely nothing I can do about it for now! I can't call my brothers and talk it through with them. I can't get a forensics crew up here to sweep the cabin. I've spent my entire life wanting to catch the man who hurt my sister. I'm now the closest I've ever been to answers and never felt more helpless."

She didn't answer. If anything, she looked sick with worry. *Help me, Lord. I took the risk of trusting her. I've never felt this weak before.*

"I apologize for getting loud and I'm sorry to put the weight of all this on you." He stopped pacing and turned toward her. "But right now, you're all I've got. I'm scared. I'm confused. I'm worried. I'm angry…" He shrugged, feeling the pain sear through his arm as he did so. "More than anything, I just need to know you believe me. Because I've never felt so lost."

There. That was as honest as he could be. It might even be the most gut-wrenchingly honest he'd ever been with anyone about his emotions, including his brothers. For a long moment, she didn't say anything. Defiance filled her form, and her stance made him think of a cornered boxer about to strike. *I don't know what else to do. I don't know what else to say.* Then her lips moved in what he thought was silent prayer and then as he watched the tension dropped from her form like a flower reopening after a storm. She walked over to him, tilted her head and looked up at him.

"I'm sorry too," she said. "You're going through something unimaginably horrible right now, and the last thing you need is somebody arguing with or yelling at you."

His mouth opened but something tightened in his throat, stealing the air from his lungs even if he had been able to find words.

"I believe you," she said. "I do. I know you're telling the truth about your sister, and the locket, and the facts of the situation. It's the whole situation we're stuck in that I'm struggling to make sense of too. You're not lost. At least, if you are, you're not alone."

He nodded. The tightening in his throat moved into his chest, until he seemed to feel his heart catch with every beat. He didn't say anything; neither did she. Instead, they just stood there in the darkness, face-to-face and chest to chest, so close that if they each moved their heads, just a little, their lips would touch. And the sudden unexpected and inexplicable realization that something inside him very much wanted that to happen sent an unexpected shiver up his spine.

"I'm feeling really angry, scared and confused too," she said. Her arms parted, so did his, and she stepped up to lean into his chest, slowly and tentatively like she was just as unused to hugging someone outside of family as he was. She wrapped her arms around him. He hugged her back as tightly as he could with one arm and felt her shiver against his chest. He held her there, feeling the warmth of her filling his core and bracing each other against the cold. Her shivering stopped and after a long moment, she stepped away.

She walked over to her phone and picked it up.

"Still no signal," she said. "And the battery's down to almost nothing. We should keep it off. Probably should turn the flashlight off too to save battery power."

"Agreed," he said. Did his voice sound as strange to her as it did to him? If anything, the lump in his throat was bigger than it had been before the unexpected hug and now he had to push his words past it. "Hopefully we'll be able to get a signal once the storm clears. There's no point trying as long as the rain's this bad. But this cabin's at a pretty high altitude, and I know a few other tricks for boosting a signal. Worse case scenario, I'll go sit on the roof. You can sleep if you want. I'm not going to sleep until we're safely out of these woods and back in the real world."

The real world. Now why had he called it that?

"Thank you," Grace said. "But I don't think I'll be able to sleep. I'd suggest we take turns keeping watch, but I don't imagine you'll be able to sleep either."

No, neither did he. He did another quick check around the cabin for vulnerabilities, while Grace held the flashlight for him. Then they switched the light off and sat down by the door in the darkness, back to back, and listened to the rain.

"My brother's getting married the day after tomorrow," he said, after a long moment, "as you probably know. It would be really great to have some answers by then."

"I heard the wedding's at a big estate near Huntsville," Grace said. He felt her back brush gently against his and somehow it felt just as intimate as their hug had been.

"Yeah," he said. "When my parents gave Trent and Chloe some money toward the wedding, they gave the rest of us an equal amount. I figured I wasn't the marrying kind, so bought myself a motorcycle. It's a really sweet one."

He chuckled. Grace did too.

Then he felt his smile fade. "I don't know how I'm ever going to tell them about this."

Silence fell between them again.

"I remember reading about your sister's death," Grace said after a long moment. He felt her back brush gently against his. "I read the news obsessively back then. Every morning I'd read the front page of every paper in the newspaper boxes by my bus stop, and then when I got on the bus I'd pick up every discarded newspaper I could find and take it with me. I actually got my first byline when I was fifteen. It was a letter I wrote to the editor about traffic not stopping for people crossing the road."

She chuckled slightly at the memory and leaned farther into him. He'd never imagined another person's back could fit so comfortably against his. "Your sister's story really hit me because we were about the same age. We prayed for your family in church. I'd forgotten that until just now. I prayed for you all on my own too, back when I believed prayer would do something."

"Sometimes prayer doesn't change the world around us. It just changes us," Jacob said. "I don't know if I've ever really known that other people, that strangers, were praying for us. But my mom and dad have always been big on praying for the people they see in trouble on the news. They'd been praying for my sister-in-law Daisy hours before they discovered why she was on the run from police or that my brother Max was helping her and baby Fitz. Intellectually, I know sometimes news coverage is a necessary evil because it warns people of danger or gets people to call in with leads. But until right now, I've never even stopped to think that it pushes people to pray."

"I don't blame you," she said. "I know this doesn't make it any better, but we also talked about it in school. We had a special assembly about self-defense. There are probably a lot of women who are alive today or who survived things because of your sister's death…" Her voice trailed off for a moment, as she seemed to catch herself. "I'm sorry, that probably sounds horrible. I didn't mean to imply there's ever anything good about what happened…"

"Hey, it's okay." He reached back and felt for her hand in the darkness, without looking, without thinking, like somehow he knew where it would be. Her hand slipped into his, their fingers linked. He squeezed her hand tightly. "It's okay to acknowledge that sometimes good can come out of the most horrible things."

She didn't answer. Instead, she squeezed his hand back, hard.

"That's something I believe and hold on to," he said. "That God can make new life and beauty out of ashes. That God makes incredible things come out of the worst places."

He felt her shift, but she didn't let go of his hand and he didn't let go of hers.

"You pray a lot," she said eventually. "Like a lot, a lot. It reminds me of my mother. She never stopped praying no matter what life threw at her. She wasn't married when I was born and my father dumped her when she told him she was pregnant."

"I'm sorry."

"Thanks." Her hand stayed linked in his. "She married a really wonderful guy when I was two and he's been an amazing stepfather to me. I grew up going to church with them. But it was hard. There was a lot of gossip about the fact that my mother wasn't married when I was born. A lot of rumors swirled around about my birth. My mother just raised her head high, ignored it all and said it was nobody's business but ours. She's this incredible woman, strong and independent, and people spread the worst gossip about her. Looking back, maybe it was only two or three women who gossiped about my mom, but it trickled down to their kids who were my age, and it's funny how sometimes a handful of people can feel like *everyone*. When I was sixteen, this guy I really liked asked me out. Then his mom made him take it back, because I wasn't good enough for him. I can't imagine how much worse it would've been if they'd known my dad was in jail."

He felt her shrug.

"I supposed most kids in my situation would've become rebellious," she said. "But I went the other way. I worked as hard as I could to be stronger, healthier, more successful, get the best grades and prove I could be a better person than them without God." Silence moved between them again. But it was a comfortable silence. Warm and expectant, like the air before a gentle summer rain. Then she said, "I said I was an atheist. But it's more like I was so angry at the church, my father and everyone that I couldn't pray. So I can't imagine going through everything you went through and still be praying."

He let his thumb run over her fingers, slowly and gently. He didn't know why there was something so comforting about her being there. He just knew he wasn't ready to let go.

"I'm not sure why I never shut God out of my life after what happened to Faith," he admitted. "I know I yelled at God a lot. I screamed in fury. I prayed a lot of hurt and angry prayers. But I figure that if God's real, and God's there, and God's listening, then I'm going to pray."

He wasn't sure if that was a good enough answer. But it was an honest one. They lapsed back into silence and after a while, he felt her hand slip from his.

"I'm sorry I didn't get a better look at the man who ambushed us," she said. "It was dark, and he was wearing a mask. But I did manage to bash him pretty hard on the side of his head, so he should have a nasty gash there. I couldn't begin to guess if it was Cutter or Driver."

"Or Turner," Jacob added. "Any one of the three of them could have planted the locket."

There was a long pause, and he could only guess what was going on in Grace's mind.

"You wanted to look at facts," Grace said. "So let's look at facts. Cutter and Driver are both violent offenders who have a history of assault. But Cutter specifically has assaulted women and would've been in his thirties when…when we were teenagers." He noticed she'd been careful not to mention his sister and appreciated it. "Whereas Driver would've been around nine or ten. So, unless Driver planted the locket for some reason, he's out."

"Agreed," Jacob said. "And Turner was in his forties, so it could be him."

She bristled and pulled away. "Turner pulled a trigger but never physically assaulted anyone. And those deaths were directly related to his bribery and corruption charges."

"He's still a killer," Jacob said, "who killed his partner and an informant."

"Which doesn't fit the pattern of this crime."

"As far as we know," Jacob said. He didn't even bother trying to hide the contempt in his voice. "He never confessed or took any responsibility for his actions. He didn't just go to jail protesting his innocence. He claimed some shadowy organization inside senior law enforcement had set him up, while providing zero evidence to back that up. He called them The Elders and implied they were incredibly senior officers."

"You seem to know a lot about the case considering you were a teenager when he was arrested," she said.

"I was sixteen," Jacob said. "I was already training to be a cop when he eventually went to trial. It was all anyone could talk about. Then there was appeal after appeal. What he did didn't just affect the police back then. He basically smeared the entire profession for years to anyone who would listen just to try to save himself from the consequences of his own actions. Maybe I took it a bit personally, because he'd thrown away everything I cared about. But I suspect a lot of cops feel the same way. For all we know, there was something more in the warehouse he was trying to hide than just evidence of his drug business."

"That last part was speculation," Grace said. "I thought we agreed to stick to facts."

Although he couldn't tell for sure in the darkness, something about the way she shuffled made him think she'd crossed her arms. He looked over his shoulder but couldn't see much of anything in the dark. "Fair enough."

Especially considering there wasn't anything he could do about it and there was no point getting himself frustrated now.

"Do you think there's any possibility that Turner was set up by a group of dirty cops?" Grace asked.

"No, I don't." Jacob shook his head. "Because if something like that was going on, more people would know about it and there'd be evidence. Nothing stays hidden forever."

She didn't answer. After a while, he felt the floorboards shift as she stretched out on the floor. He lay on his back beside her, feeling the cold hardwood beneath him, not knowing if she was asleep or awake, and listened to the storm, her breath, any sign someone might be lurking outside and the beating of his own heart.

Time passed and after a while they started talking again in whispered tones. Not about crime or killers, but lighter topics, like the music they enjoyed, concerts they'd gone to, books they'd read and places they wanted to travel. They talked for hours, lying a few feet apart on the cold wooden floor, like children whispering on a camping sleepover. Until slowly, finally, the rain died down to a gentle patter before fading off completely, the wind stopped and rays of the August morning sun began to slip through the cracks in the door and the window toward them.

They sat up slowly and exchanged smiles. Grace curled herself into a tight ball, then slowly unwound and stood.

"Good morning." A smile crossed her lips and filled her eyes. She reached out a hand toward him; he took it and let her help pull him up. "Looks like we survived the night."

"Yeah." He dropped her hand and ran his own through his hair. He wasn't sure what to make of the fact that things had been so quiet—almost too quiet—and there hadn't been so much as a rustle in the bushes. "Mind if I try your phone again now that the storm's died down? If it's all the same to you, I'd like to give rescue a shout and see just how quickly they can get a helicopter out here to pick us up. The sooner we can get out of these woods the better. Want to go grab coffee together after the helicopter ride but before we go our separate ways?"

She bit her lip slightly as she smiled and suddenly it hit him that his last comment had sounded an awful lot like he'd just asked her out on a date, which hadn't been what he'd meant at all. He'd just meant they were both really tired and needed caffeine, so they might as well drink some after the helicopter dropped them off but before she made her way back to Toronto. Once they got back, he'd then need to rush off to coordinate a team to search the cabin, contact Liam about retrieving that additional evidence and, of course, give Trent a call to let him know he was sorry he'd missed the bachelor party but would be there tonight for the rehearsal and definitely wouldn't miss the wedding tomorrow. After all, when Grace had emailed him and suggested they grab coffee, that hadn't been a date, right?

"Coffee sounds pretty amazing." A smile crossed her lips and dazzled in her eyes.

She reached into her bag, pulled out two protein bars and handed him one. Then she shook the canteen. "You're probably going to want a couple of minutes of privacy to make your phone calls and I'm thirsty. If I remember correctly, there's a stream just a few feet from the cabin. Any objection if I go refill the canteen and splash some water on my face?"

He shook his head. "No, just stay vigilant, stay within eyesight of the cabin and if you hear me shout, answer right away."

"Got it." She unlocked the door and swung it open. Rising sun flooded in. Water glistened from the trees. Puddles covered the ground, but the sky was cloudless, streaked with blue and pink from the sunrise. He checked his watch. It was almost five thirty in the morning and the storm was over. *Thank You, God.* Rescue would hopefully be on their way any minute. "See you in a bit."

"Wait." Jacob hesitated. Then he reached down and pulled the gun she'd lifted off Cutter from his ankle holster. He held it out to her. "Take this. Don't fire it unless you have to."

Her fingers brushed his as she took the weapon from his hand. Her eyes lingered on his face. "Thank you."

"No problem."

She slid the gun into her belt, covered it with her jacket and then saluted. "See you back here in five."

"Yeah, see you then."

Grace stepped out into the sunshine. The phone was showing half a signal bar. Jacob removed the case then climbed up onto the roof to boost the signal even more. He braced his feet against a skylight and shot off a quick text to his brother Trent's secure phone line using the short-form code words they'd established years ago to let the fellow detective know it was him, to call him back and that the line was unsecured. Then he prayed the phone would keep its battery long enough for Trent to call him back. He didn't know either Kevin or Warren's numbers off by heart and while calling his division would eventually get him patched into local Search and Rescue efforts, his brother Trent would be way more efficient. Plus, if he only had enough juice for one phone call, he knew whose voice he wanted to hear and was going to make that one call count.

He watched as Grace disappeared into the trees and he lost sight of her through the dense foliage. He felt almost self-conscious watching her go. Had he done the right thing in giving her back the weapon? There'd been a moment between them—or more like a whole string of moments—since he'd dropped down between the rocks to save her. That sense he'd had that they were like magnets pulling together and pushing apart hadn't faded once in the hours they'd spent together and if anything, the pull was getting stronger. All too soon, they'd be back in the real world. Her life would go back to normal. His life would continue, even though he suspected it would take a long time to feel *normal* again. What would that mean for the burgeoning of whatever there was between him and Grace? Would she keep sending him emails and would he keep ignoring them? Would they start nodding politely to each other in passing at crime scenes?

Would he ask her out for coffee? Would he let his hand reach across the table for hers?

The phone in his hand rang, the sound seeming to shatter the peaceful silence of the morning. He glanced at the screen—*Thank You, God!*—then snapped the phone to his ear.

"Hey, Trent!" he said. "I'm sorry I missed the bachelor party!"

"I'm sure you are!" His younger brother's voice boomed back down the phone with more than a hint of a relieved laugh in it. There was nobody else he knew who was capable of sounding that wide-awake before six in the morning. "Tell me you've got a good excuse."

"I got shot." Jacob braced his feet against the roof, leaned back and stared up at the sky. "Then I fell from a Search and Rescue helicopter, nearly drowned and got stranded in Algonquin."

Not that Trent, his brother and a fellow RCMP detective, wouldn't pretty much already know most of that.

But it never hurt to remind him for future Henry brothers bragging rights.

"I spoke to Detective Warren Scott this morning," Trent said, making Jacob wonder just how long his brother had been awake and how much of the day before his wedding had already been spent on making sure Jacob was safe. "Short call. Your pilot from yesterday came down with some kind of severe food poisoning. Nasty stuff. Spread through Search and Rescue. A lot of the team are grounded. A few have been hospitalized. Considering the large-scale efforts now underway to get roads reopened, power lines back up and people rescued after last night's storm, the timing couldn't be worse. Law enforcement are really stretched. Once the airport reopens, they'll be flying in RCMP from across the country to help out. But Warren told me a bird would be in the air soon and reaching you by six."

Sounded like they needed him to get out of the woods and help out.

"Now, what's the situation with you?" Trent asked.

Jacob quickly filled him in on everything that had happened with Cutter, Driver and the unknown attacker in the cabin. Trent whistled.

"But that was hours ago," Jacob added. "We had no trouble in the night and they could be anywhere now."

"Yeah, and I didn't know all that," Trent said. "For whatever reason, that information is being kept close to the chest. I can only assume they're mobilizing ground troops to search the woods. But again, the storm last night was brutal. We're talking a massive blackout, downed trees taking out power lines, and closed roads. It's pretty bad. So, again, we're stretched pretty thin."

"Understood," Jacob said. If it weren't for his brother's wedding, he'd have insisted on joining the ground search for the escaped convicts as soon as he was sure Grace was safely heading back to Toronto.

"Just stay safe," Trent said. "Keep your head down and watch your back."

"Will do."

"And promise me you're going to be there for the rehearsal dinner tonight." Now a teasing grin hovered in his brother's voice. "Not that I didn't know when I asked you to be my best man that I was running the risk of something like this happening."

"Har, har," Jacob said. "I'll be there. Just pray for me, okay? We've still got to get out of here alive. Hopefully though it won't be much longer."

He took a deep breath and debated whether to tell his brother about the locket. He needed to tell Trent. He needed to tell his entire family. But should he just blurt it out on a phone call? Should he wait until after the wedding? He tucked the phone into the crook of his neck, reached into his pocket and felt for the locket.

He ran the smooth chain through his fingers. One way or another, this was the kind of thing he needed to tell them in person.

"So your civilian is Grace Finch?" Trent asked.

Jacob sat up straight. "How do you—?"

"Call display," Trent said. "Not that I didn't trace the number as well before I called it. She's the reporter from *Torchlight News*, right? The one you get all tongue-tied and red-faced around?"

Jacob had forgotten Trent had been at a handful of the crime scenes when Grace had approached him, and didn't much like his brother describing his reaction as either red-faced or tongue-tied.

"She's a brave and brilliant woman," Jacob said. With a softer heart than he'd imagined.

"And?" Trent pressed.

"And I should go find her." Jacob scanned the trees. He hadn't laid eyes on her in almost five minutes and that was long enough. "I'll call you from the helicopter or as soon as I can after we land."

"Wait," Trent said. "There's something I need to tell you. And I was going to wait until you got back, but it doesn't feel right."

Yeah, Jacob kind of knew the feeling. "What's up?"

Trent took a deep breath, like he was debating how to put what he needed to say.

"Liam Bearsmith got made," Trent said. "Somehow his cover got blown. He went to meet you, obviously you weren't there, something went wrong and he was shot in the parking lot."

Jacob took in a sharp breath. *Lord, I should've been there.*

"He's alive," Trent added. "But he's in a coma. The bullet went into his skull and doctors don't know if he's ever going to wake up again."

A weight, huge and invisible, seemed to press against Jacob's chest. Liam had risked his life to tell Jacob what he'd discovered about Faith. And now he was fighting for his life.

Lord, please have mercy on Liam. Spare his life.

"Whatever evidence he might've been carrying about Faith's attacker's DNA has been lost," Trent said. "Police and paramedics didn't find anything on him. Not a wallet, a laptop, a thumb drive or a phone. He was considered a John Doe for almost an hour before police figured out he was one of ours."

"How…how was his cover blown?" Jacob demanded. *Lord, is this my fault?*

"No idea," Trent said. "But for now it seems our only lead to what happened to Faith is gone."

The locket sat heavier in Jacob's pocket. No, not the only lead. "Trent, I'm sorry to do this to you the day before your wedding, but there's something I've got to tell you too…"

Then he heard the muffled cry coming from the woods behind the cabin, like someone had tried to shout only to be silenced.

"Don't move and don't scream, kiddo, I'm not going to hurt you." The voice in Grace's ear was rough, low and all too familiar. She wasn't sure how her father had gotten the jump on her from behind, but there was no doubt whose hand it was clamped over her mouth. "I'm not going to hurt you, kiddo. I promise. I just want to talk."

Everything inside her recoiled. He had no right to call her *kiddo* once, let alone twice, and she knew just how little his promises were worth. Her father's arm around her was both familiar and foreign at once. Growing up, his hugs had always felt awkward and uncomfortable, and yet she'd craved them as if somehow, if they just shared the right hug, at the right time, everything would be fixed and they'd start having a normal father-and-daughter relationship. Then he went to jail and there was nothing but radio silence for so long that her father became a footnote in her life. Then came his first letter and his second, until finally she found herself sitting across from him again, talking to him through Plexiglas.

Something sharp pressed against her throat from behind. A knife? A piece of glass? She didn't know. Whatever it was, it wasn't a gun. Did that mean he didn't have one and he hadn't been the one who'd fired off his gun in the cabin the night before?

Her hands itched to grab her own gun.

"Grace? Hey, Grace?" She could hear Jacob's voice coming from somewhere behind her. "You okay?"

No, Jacob couldn't find her like this. She needed to fix this. She needed to sort this out. Then once she got her head around what was going on, she'd tell Jacob everything.

"Tell him you're fine," her father said.

"Give me a minute!" she shouted back. "I'm…" *I'm fine!* The words hovered on her lips and she barely kept herself from saying them. No, she wasn't going to lie to Jacob. Not now. Not after everything they'd been through. "I'm just taking care of something."

Could the fear and tension she was feeling show?

"Enough of this," she said, her voice feeling as cold and dull as metal. "Let me go. Now."

"I'd love to, kiddo, but I can't do that just yet," her dad said. "Because there's some really important stuff I need to tell you. Now, you've got to promise not to yell."

No, he was done being the one giving the orders.

"Really? And what are you going to do if I scream? Choke me? Strangle me? Is that the kind of thing you do?" The words flew from her lips as sharp and sudden as a whip's crack, and she felt his grip weaken from their impact. She grabbed the hand at her throat with both of hers, pealing the sharp object away from her skin and kicking back hard. He let go. She spun around to face him.

It had been how many years since her last prison visit? A handful? He looked older than she remembered. His beard was scraggly and the last of his hair had gone from a mix of red and gray to white. His skin was paler too, with almost a translucent quality to it that made his blue eyes stand out even more. He was still as tall and broad as he'd ever been, but now his shoulders were hunched like a vulture's. A rolled up wool hat sat low over his hair. If she yanked off his hat, would she see the wound her flashlight had made on whoever had charged at her in the room last night?

She stepped back, her hands instinctively rising to strike, as her fingers tightened on the object she'd wrenched from his hand. It was smooth and felt like plastic. Her hand shook. "Tell me, *Dad*, what exactly are you going to do if I don't cooperate? Shoot at me like you did last night?"

"Hey! No need for all that! I wasn't going to try anything. I promise!" His now-empty hands rose, palms up. Right, like he'd promised if she'd just deposit five thousand dollars into a joint bank account he'd set up and didn't ask where the money went, he wouldn't ask for any more. Then he asked for another thousand, and another, and another, and told her that if she stopped paying, he'd leak to the press that Canada's top crime reporter was secretly the daughter of a criminally convicted dirty cop. "And I don't even have a gun. I promise."

He didn't? It was only then she actually stopped and looked down at the item she was holding. It was a plastic toothbrush sharpened to a fine point. She'd given him that toothbrush, in one of the care packages he'd asked her for because he said his teeth were sensitive because he was getting old. Then he'd turned it into a weapon and held it to her throat.

"Hey, Grace!" Jacob's voice grew louder and more urgent. Seemed he'd climbed down off the cabin roof and was coming her way. "Where are you?"

She didn't answer. Instead, as she stared down at the shiv, a rush of anger swept over and through her heart, and it took all the self-control in her body not to physically reach out and hit him.

"Did you kill Faith Henry?" her voice seethed. "Did you actually kill a girl? Is that why you lured me here? Is that why her locket was in the cabin? Is that what you wanted me to find? She was my age! She was innocent! She had nothing to do with your drug enterprise, and your corruption, whatever illegal and underhanded schemes you had for making money!"

"Are you out of your mind?" He leaped back. His voice rose so loud she was worried Jacob would hear him. "Of course I didn't kill a girl! I didn't kill anybody! Ever! I told you! I was—"

"Framed!" She finished the sentence before he could. "By *The Elders*, a group no one has ever had any proof existed. I know, my poor, poor innocent good cop father who never did anything wrong. Whose bank account was full of dirty money, whose partner and informant got shot and whose DNA just happened to show up on the murder weapon because people were out to get him!"

Her hand hovered as if to push him back. His hand hovered as if to pull her closer. But neither moved.

"Yeah!" he said, his eyes wide, with that innocent look that might've once fooled her mother but not a jury of his peers. "I am innocent of everything. Everything. I was framed!" Like almost every other criminal whose trial she'd sat through. "I definitely didn't kill any girl!"

"Grace! Where are you?" Worry filled Jacob's voice.

"That's a cop, isn't it?" Her father's voice quickened, his limbs shaking with that old familiar agitation of a man who was itching to run. "You can't trust the cops, kiddo. You can't. That's what I'm here trying to tell you. The same cops who framed me, did those crimes and shot those people are coming after you now. Because they don't like the stories you've been writing. They're very high up, they're very connected and they're coming for you. They're behind all of this and they're going to kill you!"

EIGHT

Had her father, the criminal, just stood there after escaping prison and insisted that not only had he been framed by some dirty cops, over twenty years ago, they were now out to kill her? Was that the best he could come up with? Then another sound filled her ears, a low and steady thrum, like thunder filling a blue and cloudless sky. A Search and Rescue helicopter was coming.

"Come on," she said. "You're going to come with me and turn yourself in, and we're going to get on that helicopter and get out of these woods."

"You can't!" His head shook. "You step foot on that helicopter, they'll kill you. They'll frame you for crimes after you're gone and frame somebody you care about for your death."

She had to go. Jacob was looking for her.

"Stop it!" she said. "Why did you really lure me to this cabin?"

"I didn't!" Turner said. "I promise! A friend of mine, a guard who does me favors in exchange for things, passed me a letter from someone anonymous telling me The Elders were going to lure you here and kill you, unless I got here to stop it!"

"And where's the letter now?" she asked.

"I destroyed it!"

"Of course you did."

"It told me all about the prison van break," he said. "When it would happen, where guns had been hidden in the van, what I should do, where to go once the van crashed and that I should pass the information on to Cutter and Driver so they'd be prepared. It even told me to bring a shiv and that I wouldn't be searched. They told how to find this cabin. They planned it all!"

"Who? The secret people who framed you? You've given me no proof they exist!"

"Grace! Answer me! Please!" Jacob's voice called. She heard him coming through the trees toward them.

"Jacob! I'm here!"

All this foolishness ended now. Let Turner tell his ridiculous story to Jacob.

And keep her secret? Or expose it?

Either way, he'd never look at her the same again...

Her father turned as if to run. In an instant, she snapped the gun from her belt, held it aloft and trained it on him.

"Stop! Right there! Or I'll shoot you."

Her father turned back. His hands were half raised. "You won't shoot me, kiddo. You're too weak-hearted like your mother."

"Are you sure about that?" Was she? She'd never aimed a gun at anyone before, let alone shot anyone before. "Tell me, did you kill that girl?"

"No!" His head shook. "I promise. I never laid a hand on any child, any woman, ever. I have my faults, but that's not one of them."

She believed him on that. But she didn't know why, and she wasn't about to trust her gut. The helicopter grew louder.

"Prove it!" she shouted over the sound of the rotors.

"I can't!" he said.

"Prove you're innocent. Prove to me that you were set up. Prove The Elders exist!"

"You just gotta believe me!"

How? Based on what? With what evidence? The helicopter kept roaring, mingled with the sound of Jacob calling her name. Jacob sounded so close. In any second he'd find them.

Her father was backing away. His head was shaking. "I gotta go! But don't get on the helicopter! And don't trust any cops!"

"Stop!" She raised the weapon. "I can't let you go!"

"You won't shoot me in the back, kiddo," he said. "You're too good for that."

Her father turned and ran. She raised her weapon. Tears flooded her gaze. Her finger shook on the trigger. Turner disappeared, deeper and deeper into the woods.

"Grace!" Jacob exploded though the forest beside her. "What happened? Are you all right? Why is your gun out? Didn't you hear me calling? I told you not to disappear like that!"

She turned to him. Tears spilled down her cheeks. Her father had been there, and she'd let him get away. Was she really that weak?

"What happened?" Jacob's green eyes searched her face. "Was somebody here? Did somebody hurt you?"

She opened her mouth, but no words came out, instead just hot embarrassing tears were coursing down her cheeks. She had to tell Jacob everything. He had to know. But she had no idea how.

"Come on," Jacob said. He turned to leave. "We have to go. You can tell me about it when we're on the helicopter or when we're grabbing that coffee. We're almost out of here."

Once she told Jacob everything about her father—from why she was in the woods to the fact that she'd just seen Turner, to what he'd told her and that she was his child—Jacob would never, ever look at her the same way again. Even if he kept her secret, she'd lose his respect.

Help me, Lord! A prayer, sudden and unexpected, filled her heart. *Can I trust him?*

"Wait!" She stepped in front of him. Her hand pressed up against his chest. "What we say here stays here, right? That was the deal last night? That's what we agreed to? That whatever we told each other couldn't be repeated to anyone?"

She looked up into his face, but the warm, soft, honest and unguarded eyes of last night were gone. Now all she saw were the eyes of a cop, with a job to do.

"What's wrong?" he asked. "What's going on?"

"We can't get on that helicopter," she said. "You can't signal them, and you can't call any cops until we've talked."

Not that she believed her father. Not that he had any credibility. But if there was even the tiniest sliver or truth to what her father had said…

"Why?" Jacob's gaze locked onto hers. "Why can't we get on that helicopter? What's going on, Grace?"

She took a deep breath. Was she really about to tell

someone the truth about her father? Was she really about to tell someone the secret she'd been keeping about her identity her entire life?

"Somebody told me that this whole thing was set up by a group of dirty cops who are trying to kill me."

He would've laughed if the whole situation weren't so deadly serious.

"You mean like The Elders?" He heard his own voice grow colder, deeper and sharper, into what he thought as his cop voice. "What are you talking about, Grace? Who told you that?"

What did she know? What hadn't she told him? *Why did I ever trust her?* He felt himself taking a step backward.

"First, you've got to promise me that whatever I tell you about myself isn't going to be reported or repeated…"

"No, I can't promise you that."

"But… Please… Jacob, I need you to listen. I need you to understand. I'm taking the biggest risk of my life trusting you…"

Her head was shaking. Her dark eyes were pleading for something he couldn't give. His heart raced, taking his breath along with it. He knew that tone of voice all too well. It was the type of voice he'd learned to lean in and listen to. It was the voice of someone who knew something they didn't want him to know. It was a tone that sounded an awful lot like guilt and a bit like dread. Suspicion crawled up inside his core, preparing his ears for whatever confession she was about to make.

His eyes searched the face of the beautiful, incredible, dazzling woman who just hours earlier had seemed to fit so comfortably in his arms.

"Grace?" He felt his voice sharpen, his words dropping as slowly and deliberately as if they were pieces of evidence he was laying out on a witness table in the interrogation room. "Tell me. Now."

"I never lied to you." Her chin rose. Gone now were the tears from her eyes, replaced with the focus of a fighter entering the ring. "Everything I've told you has been true, even if I haven't told you everything I know."

"I'll be the judge of that," he said. His walkie-talkie was buzzing now. The Search and Rescue helicopter was hailing him. He holstered his weapon, told whoever was at the other end that he needed a minute and turned the volume down.

"I was telling the truth when I told you I had no idea about the prison break," she said. "Because I didn't. But I wasn't here by accident either." She was talking quickly, as if trying to get as many words out as possible before he shut her down. "I got a tip."

His eyes narrowed. "What kind of tip?" he asked. "From who?"

She swallowed a breath. "Hal Turner."

Disgust soured the taste at the back of his throat. "A dirty cop and a cop killer."

And she'd been talking to him?

Fear mingled with courage in her eyes, just as they had back before. But now he didn't know where the fear was coming from. Was she scared of the information she had? Of Hal Turner? *Of me?*

"I got a letter that was purported to be from Hal Turner—"

"When?"

"Three days ago," she said. "He gave me the location of the cabin and told me he'd left proof there that he was innocent of all the charges he'd been convicted of and somebody else had set him up."

Frustration filled his body like a wave until it felt like a physical, invisible wall pushing his heart away from hers.

How could this possibly have anything to do with Faith's locket?

"And you didn't report it to police?" Jacob asked.

"What? That a criminal had written to me saying he was innocent? Criminals behind bars and the general public contact me every day with wild and crazy criminal theories. Ninety-nine point nine percent are ludicrous and from the kind of people who've probably reported to every law enforcement unit and media outlet. If we took every single one seriously, I'd spend all day calling in tips."

"Except you chased this one out to the woods a few hours before a prison break."

"The letter said nothing about a prison break!" Her voice rose. "If it had, I'd have reported it to police immediately. It said that he was innocent of the crimes he'd been accused of and had left evidence here. Look, I'm not saying I believe he's innocent. I'm just telling you what happened. Then we get to the cabin and the only evidence we find is your sister's locket."

And how exactly did the death of a twelve-year-old girl from a small town in Ontario, whose father was a farmer and mother was a nurse, have anything to do with a dirty cop's crimes two years later and hundreds of miles away?

It didn't. It just didn't. There wasn't a theory far-fetched enough to make it so.

"You're saying Hal Turner lured you here to find my sister's locket?"

"He says he didn't send the letter and doesn't know anything about the locket!"

"When?" Jacob demanded. "When did he tell you this?"

Her eyes closed. Her lips moved in silent prayer. Then she opened her eyes again.

"Right now," she said, and it was like he could hear something strengthen in her voice. "He told me right now, not five minutes ago in the woods. That's why I wasn't calling you back. He got the jump on me and threatened me with a shiv. I took the shiv. He told me not to get in the helicopter or trust the cops because The Elders were out to kill me. Then he ran away. I tried to shoot him, but I froze."

Now the frustration that had crashed over his heart like a wave broke free of its floodgates and coursed through his veins.

"He told me he got an anonymous letter from The Elders explaining everything about the prison break before it happened," she said. "He said he destroyed the letter, but it told him the prison break was happening and everything to do!"

"Grace—"

"I'm not saying I believe him! I'm not saying I was right! I'm just telling you what happened!"

The helicopter roared louder. It was an odd noise

and a loud noise, screeching like he'd never heard before. His eyes looked up. The helicopter was spinning, looping like someone had reached up, grabbed it and spun it like a child's toy.

"Come on!" he said. His hand reached for her arm. "This isn't over, but we've got to go."

But then he watched as the helicopter plummeted, sideways, falling and spinning toward the horizon to their east.

Lord, I don't know what—

Someone tumbled from the helicopter, their body free-falling for a moment and then their parachute opened. The helicopter dropped from view and a loud and deafening bang seemed to the split the sky.

Their rescue helicopter had crashed.

NINE

The parachute hovered briefly on the horizon with a figure suspended underneath from the harness before drifting behind the trees. Jacob's heart pounded. The helicopter had crashed. It had somehow suddenly fallen from the sky. The thought pounded through Jacob's mind like a deafening heartbeat. *No! Please! God have mercy!*

Their rescue was gone, along with maybe the lives of anyone who hadn't managed to leap to safety. A fellow officer was now stranded alone in the woods. Jacob's eyes closed as panicked, desperate prayers for his colleague's safety poured from his lips. The sound of the crash seemed to echo through the forest like a bomb had gone off, mingled with the painful high-pitched screech of metal rotors still fighting to spin against rock.

Then suddenly he realized Grace was in his arms.

Had he reached for her in that moment of fear? Or had she been the one to step up against his chest? He had no idea. All he knew was that his one good arm was tightening around her, pulling her in so close that as his lips moved in prayer he felt them brush over her head. Her arms were around him. Her hands clutched his back. The gentle murmur of prayers flowed from Grace's lips. She prayed that everyone who'd been on board had managed to leap before the crash and were now safe. He closed his eyes and prayed with her for God's mercy.

Then silence fell.

The bang faded, the screech of the rotors stopped, and for a moment, the vacuum of sound it left was so quiet that it was like they'd been plunged into total silence. Slowly, the normal sounds of running water, wind in the trees and their own ragged breaths began to return to their ears. They untangled slowly and pulled out of each other's arms.

The fear and panic that filled Grace's eyes were a mirror of what he felt in his own. And he felt everything important they needed to talk about, even needed to argue about, recede for now to the back of his mind.

"Tell me they survived the crash, Jacob. Please, tell me whoever was in that helicopter survived the crash." Her words came out are barely more than a whisper.

"I saw someone leap with a parachute," he said, and although they were stepping back, he felt his hand reach for hers and squeeze it tightly. "I don't know if there was anyone else on board. But my brother Max and sister-in-law Daisy survived a pretty hairy helicopter crash once, in the same type of Search and Rescue helicopter."

"How did this even happen?" Her voice shook. "How does a helicopter just plummet like that?"

How did it, Lord? I don't know. And I wish I did.

"Maybe there was a mechanical malfunction," he said. "That's the most obvious explanation."

The skies had been clear, without so much as a cloud. The idea that somebody was hiding out in the woods with the kind of weapon that would take down a helicopter was ludicrous and besides, he'd have seen the attack. No, this was more like the helicopter had just stopped flying and fallen from the sky.

"It could also have been a medical emergency," he admitted. "Trent, my brother, said that a random illness swept over the Search and Rescue team last night," he said slowly and almost as if to himself. "Something like severe food poisoning, only worse. They were shipping RCMP in from other provinces to help with rescue efforts. But with the storm shutting the major airports, everything is taking so much longer. I... I don't know how long it will be until another helicopter will be sent. But they will be sending rescue. Both to the helicopter crash site and for us."

A sudden unsettling suspicion tickled at the back of his mind, as the thoughts he'd pushed away about Hal Turner, The Elders and the fight they'd been having right before the crash began to clamor to be heard. His brain felt whiplashed, pushing away from Grace whenever he realized he couldn't trust her, and then finding himself inexplicably pulled back to her again. But he couldn't ignore the fact that Turner had told Grace that corrupt cops were out to kill her. And even though not a single iota of evidence had ever been found to prove that The Elders were anything more than one criminal's desperate lie and fantasy story, he didn't much like the fact that a convicted criminal had warned Grace not to get on the helicopter minutes before it crashed.

"We have to get there," Grace said, her words coming out short and fast. "We have to get to the crash site, find whoever leaped out and see if there's anything we can do."

"It's miles away," he said. "It will take hours, and if we leave here it might take longer for rescue to find us."

But even as he felt his head shake, he knew she was right. He owed it to those he served with to try and make it there.

"There will be medical supplies on the helicopter, right?" Grace added. "And a radio, a phone and other supplies?"

"You're right," he said.

"We can get there faster if we take my canoe. Hopefully it survived the storm. The river will be swollen from the rain but—"

He squeezed her hand tightly. "I said you're right. We're going to go to the helicopter crash site and see if we can find whoever leaped. Right now." Relief visibly flooded her form. He pulled his hand from hers. Then he turned away and reached for her borrowed cell phone. "I just need to make a quick call as we walk."

"Wait." Her hand grabbed his arm before he could dial. "What about The Elders?"

"The Elders don't exist," he said sharply. "They're a myth and a ludicrous conspiracy theory invented by a selfish and narcissistic crook to try to cover for the fact that he extorted criminals, turned a blind eye to the dealers who paid him and killed two people. He ruined the reputation of cops across the country, which led to dozens of criminals he'd put away appealing their convictions. Some even got out! I've served with cops who saw the investigations they worked on get shredded in the courts and the criminals they helped put away set free only to reoffend. Hal Turner spat on the badge and sold out everything we believe in. *To serve and protect.* That's the Toronto police motto he signed on for. He did neither and betrayed both."

A breeze moved through the morning air. Grace pulled her hand away from his arm.

"You hate him, don't you?" Grace asked. "Turner. You really hate him."

"I don't hate him," Jacob said automatically. "I don't hate anybody."

"You hate the man who killed your sister," Grace said softly. "Nobody can blame you for that. You wouldn't be human if you weren't angry."

Okay, fair enough. But still.

"Grace," he said. "I'm a guy who believes in God and that means believing in God's forgiveness. I don't get to pick and choose who's worthy of it."

"'Be ye kind one to another, tenderhearted, forgiving one another, even as God for Christ's sake hath forgiven you...'" Grace said slowly, as if pulling the words from somewhere in her distant memory. "That's New Testament, right? My mom used to have that verse up in her bathroom, right over the mirror."

"Yup, Ephesians," he said.

"Mom always told me that forgiveness had a lot of layers," she said. "That it was a process and not something that happened all at once. She says sometimes you've got to forgive the same person for the same sin over, and over, and over again in new and deeper ways."

He wasn't sure what she meant by that, or if she was

talking about him or herself. So instead, he turned to the phone.

"We only have enough juice for a super quick phone call," he said, "and I'm calling the one cop I trust more than anyone else on the planet: my brother Trent."

Her head shook. "But what if it's possible, even just a little tiny bit possible, that Turner is right, and The Elders are real and there is a group of cops out there trying to kill me and frame someone for your sister's murder?"

"Look, I know you've never had a sibling," he said, turning back. "And I know that not everyone has a family as close-knit and supportive as mine. But my brother Trent and soon-to-be sister-in-law, Chloe, kept our sister-in-law Daisy safe and her identity secret when she was on the run from police. Trent coordinated with another detective under deep cover to help rescue our brother Nick and my other sister-in-law Erica from a train heist…"

His voice trailed off as suddenly another thought jolted his heart, something he'd forgotten in the chaos that had unfolded. Liam Bearsmith, the undercover detective who'd helped Nick and Erica and their son make it home alive was now lying in a coma because of whatever he knew about Faith's death.

"You okay?" Grace asked.

He blinked. "I'm as all right as I'm going to be under the circumstances. Trent told me the person who'd promised me evidence about my sister's death had his cover blown and is now lying in a coma."

"I'm so sorry." Grace's hand rose to her lips. "God have mercy on him."

"Amen," he completed her prayer. "Anyway, my

point is, if there's anyone on this planet I trust right now to help get us out of this, it's him. Besides, now I've got to explain why I might be a little bit late for his wedding rehearsal tonight."

Her canoe paddle dipped crisply and smoothly into the water, as they followed the quickly moving river through the woods. The sun sent golden flashes of light dancing over the surface as the swollen river wound its way around fallen trees, rockslides and debris. Broken branches and split trunks punctuated the woods on either side. The storm had been devastating. She'd felt a closeness with Jacob, a connection, a trust that she'd never felt with anyone before. But when the storm had ended, her father had gotten the jump on her and the helicopter had crashed…

Her head shook as a dozen conflicting emotions flooded through her core.

And now they were canoeing, together, with her in the bow and Jacob in the stern. He'd barely spoken a word since his short phone conversation with his brother. From the snippets she'd been able to catch, Jacob had been really blunt and direct with him about everything that had happened and what she'd told him. Trent had promised to look into it and do whatever he could. Then the phone had died. For now, all they could do was wait, paddle and hope they could find a phone in the helicopter crash site.

Could they really trust Trent? Could she trust Jacob? And yet whenever she looked into Jacob's eyes, she could see something there, something deep and real, that pulled her in and made her long for the type of emotional closeness and partnership she'd never felt before.

She didn't know how to begin to define what she felt for him, only that she'd never felt that way about anyone else. And what difference did it make, anyway? Even if she weren't a journalist, Jacob would never let himself get close to the daughter of a criminal he clearly despised. He'd probably forgive her for not telling him that Hal Turner was her father. Because that was the kind of good man Jacob was. But he'd never look at her the same way again.

Then suddenly another thought hit her like a well-aimed right hook: she felt safe with Jacob. Despite everything that had happened between them, she felt completely and utterly safe. Even when they were arguing, even when she was outright defying him, even when he was frustrated with her and their voices rose, she'd never once for a moment wondered if he was going to insult her or threaten her, let alone hurt her.

Somehow even while fighting with Jacob, she felt closer to him than she'd ever been to anyone she wasn't fighting with.

"I'm sorry!" she called suddenly. She glanced back over her shoulder briefly. Jacob had his paddle wedged under his injured arm and was doing the J-stroke with his left. "I'm sorry I didn't tell you about Turner. I didn't know if I could trust you. And I should have."

His green eyes were wide, but she had to turn back and face the river again before he spoke.

"I get it, I guess," he said. "You're a journalist, you had a source to protect and it's not like I'd given you a reason to think I was friendly before yesterday."

Maybe the words should've been comforting, but they weren't. It sounded like he was trying to be understanding, which wasn't the same as actually getting it.

"Let me be clear," he added, while she was still trying to figure out what to say next. "I believe that Turner sold you a big old bag of baloney. I don't believe in The Elders. I don't believe The Elders had anything to do with the prison break, or the helicopter crash, or my sister's locket showing up in the cabin. I also think you made the completely wrong call and should've told me everything sooner. I don't think you should've ever come out here into these woods. But I'm not going to hold a grudge over the fact that you made the choices you did."

Yes, but not holding a grudge wasn't the same as wanting to still grab a coffee or having anything to do with her once they left these woods. She took a deep breath.

"Do you think Turner killed your sister?" she asked.

"I think someone planted the locket shortly before we found it," he said. "And besides the two of us, Cutter, Turner and Driver are the only people we know for certain are out in these woods. And again, Driver is younger than us and was only about ten when my sister was killed, which rules him out. He doesn't fit the profile."

She sat up straighter and only realized she'd stopped paddling when she felt the tug of water threatening to pull the paddle from her hands. "You profiled the guy?"

"Not officially," he said. "But I have this idea in my head of who he is. Violent, aggressive, a repeat criminal who's probably somewhere between the ages of fifty and seventy now, I'm guessing."

Her eyes rose to the horizon. The fact that she still hadn't told him Turner was her father gnawed at her. But what would it change, really? Jacob would be leaving her life as soon as all this was over. Her father would be on the run until he was caught, and if he tried to contact her again, she'd report it to the police. There was no good reason for her to tell him.

Except the fact that something inside her wanted to. She didn't want to keep something like that from him. Even if he never looked at her the same way after, even if he never spoke to her again, she had to take the risk of opening up to him like he'd opened up to her and let him know who she really was.

"Hey!" Jacob's voice rose. "We got something up ahead!"

She glanced downriver and then she saw it, coming up all too quickly as the water carried them ever faster downstream. Smoke rose from a mass of broken treetops, bent and fractured like a giant foot had stomped on them. The stench of fuel filled the air. They rounded another corner and saw the wreckage. The helicopter lay at the water's edge, sideways and half submerged, only managing to cling to the shore by the twisted rotors wedged in between some rocks.

"Hold on!" Jacob shouted. "We're going to turn fast."

Then she felt the canoe suddenly yank beneath her. They spun quickly, tossed in the current, flying around so fast they ended up backward. She dug her paddle deep into the water, her arms straining as she paddled in deep sharp strokes toward the shore. The canoe turned.

The water beat against them, threatening to pull them away from the crash. Behind her, she could hear Jacob shouting encouragement, telling her they were going to make it and that she just had to keep paddling.

Then she felt the canoe buffet against a rock. She reached for it, held onto it tight, feeling it sharp and wet underneath her hand as Jacob steadied the boat. Then slowly and surely, using rocks and debris as a guide, they pulled and pushed their way through the water to the shore. Dirt scraped beneath them. She leaped out, splashing through the water as she pulled the canoe high enough onto the shore that Jacob could get out, as well. Then she stumbled along the shore toward the wreckage. Jacob was one step behind her.

The helicopter looked more like a broken toy than the same almost majestic aircraft she'd seen flying above them, promising rescue. The tail was snapped. The rotors were bent and twisted. Water coursed through the smashed cockpit window. There was no one to be seen.

"We have to get inside," she said. "You stay here. I'll go."

"No, I'll go." His hand landed on her arm. "It'll be a lot faster for me to scrounge up anything of value. And while the fact that it's mostly submerged should keep it from exploding, I'm not about to risk your life any more than necessary."

So much for hoping they were past this.

"Do I need to remind you you've been shot?" she asked.

"No," he said. "But need I remind you that this is my job. I'm a cop and you're—"

He caught himself before finishing the sentence. So, she finished it for him.

"A journalist," she said. "That's what you were about to say, right? Because even though I'm nowhere near my laptop and even though there isn't of pad of paper anywhere in sight, you never stop reminding me of that. Why?"

He looked down at where his hand still lay on her arm. "Maybe it's helpful for me to remember."

"Helpful how?" Her voice rose. "To remember what?"

"Not to drop my guard around you." His eyes snapped back to her face. She gasped to see just how deep the emotion floating there was. "Because no matter what, you're always going to be thinking like a journalist. We can stay up all night talking in the cabin about real stuff, and the next morning I discover you're hiding things from me and having a secret conversation with a convict in the woods for a story."

She rocked back on her heels. No, she hadn't been thinking like a journalist. She'd been thinking like a daughter. But there was no way to explain that to him now.

"You want to know why I never responded when you kept hounding me for coffee?" he asked. "Because I didn't want a reporter in my life. I didn't want someone around who treated me like nothing but a source for information and someone to be interviewed."

He started to pull his hand away from her arm, but somehow she found herself grabbing on to it, holding on to his fingers just like she had when she'd helped pull him to safety the day before.

"You think the only reason I invited you for coffee

or tried to make any connection with you back in the real world was to use you?" she asked.

Yeah, she kept telling herself that was the only reason why. But maybe she hadn't exactly been honest.

"You wanted a source within the police," he said slowly. His fingers brushed over her hand and somehow neither of them pulled away. "You wanted to build a working relationship with a cop."

"Maybe I wanted to build a working relationship with you," she said. "There are hundreds of cops in Toronto. A dozen have invited me out for coffee. And I shot them all down. Because I don't trust easily. I find it hard to make connections. I don't let people in. But you were honest and fearless. You were fundamentally good. There was something about you that made me want to get to know you better. Even if you clearly didn't want to get to know me."

There, she'd said it. She'd admitted it to herself, finally, even if blurting it out to him like that had left her feeling vulnerable and stupid. She pulled her hand away from his and crossed her arms across her chest.

"Anyway, you might be a cop, but you're also injured," she said, changing the subject before he could respond. "So, how about we find a way to work together that keeps you from potentially drowning? I have some rope in my bag. How about we tether you to a tree and you rappel in? I'll stay out here and keep watch."

Jacob didn't answer for a long moment. Instead, he just stood there, staring at her like she was a puzzle he was trying to solve in his head. He ran his hand over the rough brown scruff that traced the strong lines of his face. It looked like less of a beard and more like the need for a shave. The fact that he was still attractively rumpled and disheveled after everything they'd gone through was ridiculous.

"I'd feel more comfortable if you were a safe distance away," he said. "But I'm guessing that's not going to happen."

She felt an unexpected smile curl on her lips. "Nope, I'm going to be standing right here, with Cutter's gun in my hand, watching your back. Just like I know you'd be for me."

To her surprise he chuckled.

"What?" she asked.

"You're unbelievable," he said. "And I mean that in a good way."

He stepped toward her in the clearing, and she felt her breath tighten in her chest.

"You're also wrong." He reached for her but didn't touch her. Instead, his hand just hovered there in the air between them. She took a step toward him and felt his hand brush up against the side of her face. "Part of me very much wanted to get to know you better, but I couldn't risk it."

"Because I was a reporter."

"Because I liked you," Jacob said, "and because you were a reporter, and because I couldn't risk letting myself get too close. Not to you. Or to anybody. I still can't."

Because of his sister? Because of the responsibility he felt to his family? Either way, it didn't matter, because once he found out the truth about who her father was, he'd never look at her the same way again.

"I understand," she said. "You can't."

Even if he wanted to and she wanted to. His eyes darkened, his fingers brushed her cheek and she could tell he was thinking about kissing her. One foolish, impulsive kiss he'd immediately and forever regret.

She made the decision for him, rising on her tiptoes and letting his lips meet hers for one fleeting moment.

Then she stepped back, and his hand dropped from her face.

Had that really just happened?

She turned to her bag and rummaged inside for her rope, and for a long moment, neither of them said anything. Finally, he asked, "Are we going to talk about what just happened?"

"No." They couldn't. It didn't matter how much she liked him. They could never be together, and talking about the reasons why would only hurt them both.

"Then can you tie knots?" he asked.

"I can physically tie a knot," she said, "but maybe not the specific knots you're thinking of."

"Fair enough," he said. She stretched out the rope without meeting his eye, not even wanting to know what she'd see there. He took it. "Now, let's get to work."

Not even ten minutes later she was standing on the shore, with the rope looped around her left hand and Cutter's gun in her right, as she watched Jacob step back into the fast-moving water. Almost immediately, his legs shook as the river buffeted against him, threatening to knock him over and send him downriver. Her own feet dug deep into the ground and her legs braced. The rope grew tighter in her hands.

"You okay?" she asked.

Am I okay? Is any of this? Will I ever feel all right again?

"Yeah, yeah." His feet steadied. He glanced back over his shoulder just long enough for their eyes to almost meet. Then just as she was about to remind him to focus on where he was going, he turned back to the river. "It's just a bit more slippery than I was expecting. Now, I'm going to start making my way along the wreckage. Give me a few inches of rope for each step. Okay?"

"Will do."

He crept deeper and deeper into the raging river, using his one good hand to guide him along the hull. Finally he reached the door, grabbed the handle and, after a battle against the added weight and pressure of the water, yanked it open. He looked in. She held her breath.

"It's empty," he called after a moment that felt way too long for her liking. "There's nobody in the cockpit or the back. Hopefully the only person who was in this thing was the guy who parachuted out when the copter started failing. Now, I'm going to climb in and see what I can find. There are a couple of air pockets in here. Not too big but enough for me to gasp some air in. So I might not come out for a couple of minutes. If you need me just give the rope three sharp tugs."

"Got it."

He disappeared through the cockpit door and dove underwater before she could answer. She felt the rope tighten suddenly in her hands. Two tugs reverberated down the rope. She quickly fed him a few more inches of rope.

A twig snapped behind her. She turned and saw

nothing but leaves and branches. There was another snap, this one more like a footstep and closer. Her heart clenched in her chest as her grip tightened.

"Drop the rope and the gun!" A deep voice behind her barked. "Now!"

TEN

A figure stepped out of the woods. A cop. Or at least someone who dressed in the same dark clothes and police vest Jacob had been in the night before. The visor of his helmet covered his face. His weapon was trained on her.

"Ma'am, I'm a police officer." Authority moved through his baritone voice and something in it made her think she'd heard the voice before. "I'm not going to hurt you. But I need you to drop both your weapon and the rope and put your hands up."

Right, or he could be an escaped convict who'd somehow managed to steal an officer's clothes somewhere after the breakout and escape.

"First show me your face and give me your name and badge number!" she called. She glanced over her shoulder toward him. "And I'm not letting go of either."

She wrapped the rope around her fist, tugged three times and tightened her grip on the gun as if to make her point.

"Grace? Grace Finch?"

Warren? Detective Warren Scott shoved up the helmet of his visor with one hand. Disbelief flooded the man's voice. "Wow, I barely recognized you!"

Just how muddy and disheveled did she look?

Grace blinked. She'd run into Detective Scott at more than one crime scene. The charming detective had the kind of square jaw that counted as chiseled and had made several casual attempts of asking her out on a date before eventually getting the picture.

"What's going on here?" Jacob's voice sounded to her right. She turned. He was hanging half in and half out of the helicopter, holding onto the rope with one hand. "Warren? What are you doing here?"

"Jacob!" Warren sprinted toward the shore.

He grabbed the rope just two feet away from her, taking the weight off her arms, and wrapped it around his fist. Then he reached his other hand out over the water for Jacob. "Come on, man."

"Thanks!" Jacob clasped his fellow detective's hand and let him help him to shore. "What are you doing out here? How did you get here?"

"I was coming to get you," Warren said. "And I got most of the way in the helicopter before it completely fritzed out on me. Then I grabbed a parachute and jumped."

That would explain the parachute they'd seen. Warren dropped the rope as Jacob splashed out of the water and stumbled onto the shore.

"Was there anyone else with you?" Jacob asked. He took two steps and collapsed to his knees on the ground. He had a first aid kit in his hand and what looked like part of a radio. "Also I'm guessing you got the main radio and walkie-talkie."

"I did," Warren said. "And thankfully I was alone. This was a solo flight."

Grace pulled herself free from the rope and started for Jacob. But Warren already had him by the arm and was helping him to his feet. The two cops—the two men—stood there facing each other as if she'd temporarily vanished.

"Was this because of the food poisoning?" Jacob asked.

Warren's eyebrows rose. "Yeah… Everyone got really sick. I was sick some but okay to fly. Well, better than most so I decided to risk it."

"Any idea what caused the illness outbreak?"

"Not that I heard."

"How are you?" Jacob asked. "Any injuries?"

"Nah, I'm good. No injuries."

"Cause of the crash?" Jacob asked.

"Something mechanical." Warren shrugged. "It just stopped responding. Like a computer virus had corrupted the controls, if that is even possible."

"Have you run into any…trouble since you've landed?" Jacob asked.

Warren shook his head. "No. Thankfully. How about you?" Then he paused, as if suddenly remembering she was there. "Maybe we shouldn't talk in front of the civilian."

"This civilian has a name, Warren," Grace said, her arms crossed. "As you well know."

Warren didn't answer right away. Instead the detective looked from Jacob to her and back again.

"You two are together?" he asked Jacob.

Jacob nodded. "She's the civilian I rescued yesterday."

"I'm sorry if this puts you in an awkward position," Warren said, "but I need to ask her to surrender her weapon."

This again? Grace almost groaned.

Come on, Jacob—she urged him silently—*we've gone through too much to make me surrender my weapon again now.*

"It's not hers," Jacob said. "She took a gun off Cutter yesterday, who we assume got it off a prison guard."

Warren nodded. "I understand."

Good! Because she didn't exactly want to give it up.

"Grace?" Jacob's voice was just as soft and yet unrelentingly strong as when he'd wrapped his arms around her. But the tenderness she'd once seen in his eyes had disappeared back behind the invisible mask of being a cop. "Warren's not wrong. You know it's illegal for you to carry. I only let you have it because of extraordinary circumstances. You're safe now, with two cops."

Her jaw tightened. Everything in her heart and mind felt differently toward Detective Jacob Henry than it had just twenty-four hours ago. But to him, she was still just a reporter, a civilian, an obligation he was unexpectedly stuck with.

Jacob had called her brave once. Well, he had no idea how much courage she was summoning now.

"Okay, Jacob," she said, ignoring the other detective in the clearing and locking her gaze on Jacob's green eyes as if he were the only man there. "If you really want me to give you back the gun and go on unarmed, then I'm going to trust you. Because I figure if worst comes to worst, I'm going to be a whole lot safer with you watching my back than any attempt I make to go it alone."

His eyes widened. Slowly, she watched the softness begin to return to the depths of his eyes, like an ice barrier beginning to freeze. *Do you get what I'm saying, Jacob? Because I don't know when or if we're ever going to be alone again. And I just wanted to show you how much I respect you and that maybe I'm not the woman you think I am.* She pulled the weapon from her belt and let the trigger loop drop into her fingertips.

"I know I haven't always trusted you," she added. "And you've definitely had plenty of good reason not to trust me. But now I know the kind of man you are. I trust you. More than that, I appreciate you. Like a lot."

Appreciate. It was as close as she could get to what she was actually feeling, with Warren standing there. She admired him. She respected him. She liked him, in the deep down kind of way that when she was younger would've made her say, *Will you be my best friend?* And oh, how she was attracted to him.

Especially after that fleeing kiss.

She stepped closer, he stretched out his hand and she dropped the gun into it.

"Thank you," Jacob said. His voice dropped as he said the words and she found herself watching his lips as they moved. He slid it into his ankle holster and pulled his pant leg down over it. Then he took a step back and looked back up at Warren.

"Grace Finch," Warren started, then he sighed. "I'm really sorry to tell you this, but you're wanted for police questioning in regard to the prison break, the escape of three convicts and death of two guards."

* * *

Jacob watched as Grace's face paled. Her mouth opened and for a moment, no words came out. She looked from Warren to the sky above.

"That's ridiculous!" Jacob said. He'd never claimed to be a perfect judge of character, but something about the wringer that he and Grace had gone through in the past few hours had left him with a pretty good sense of some things. Like that she had a good heart that cared about people. And a strong mind that wouldn't willingly do something that foolish. "Grace, don't worry. I've got your back." He turned to Warren. "I don't have a clue what's been going on since I've been gone, but you and whoever's saying Grace Finch had anything to do with three killers breaking out is wrong. Grace didn't have anything to do with the prison break."

"Hey, I didn't say that she did!" Warren's shrug was so huge that his arms practically flapped. "I have a lot to fill you in on and I hate this whole situation as much as you do. But getting the civilian who's wanted for police questioning to stop illegally waving around a criminal's gun seemed like a good thing to do before the conversation continued."

Fair. But not good enough. Jacob blew out a breath. He glanced quickly at Grace to make sure he wasn't about to cut her off or talk over her. But her lips were pressed together and her arms were crossed so tightly she looked like she was trying to disappear into herself.

He just prayed she trusted him enough to let him handle this.

"Well, she's done what we've asked and handed over the weapon, and chosen to trust us…" *No… She's cho-*

sen to trust me... "Which, considering she's the one who had her life threatened, more than once, by criminals in the past twenty-four hours, is no small ask. And clearly I need to be briefed."

"In front of Grace?" Warren asked.

"We're in the middle of the woods," Jacob said. "For who knows how long. So yes, in front of Grace."

Warren rubbed his hand over the back of his neck. "We got a substantial tip from an anonymous source that Grace has been exchanging letters with Turner and she made plans to meet him in the woods, create some big false media narrative about The so-called Elders really existing, and aiding him and the other prisoners to escape."

He heard Grace's sharp intake of breath. He didn't dare look in her direction and get knocked off course again by whatever it was in her eyes that had tossed him around like the river's current when she'd told him that she trusted him. But even when he couldn't see her, he could feel her standing just off to his left. Scraps of the conversation they'd had earlier filled his mind. *You've got to promise me that whatever I tell you...isn't going to be repeated... Please... Jacob... I'm taking the biggest risk of my life trusting you...*

And he'd told her, no. That he hadn't been able promise.

"Grace has already spoken to me about the Hal Turner situation," Jacob said. "I don't believe she knew anything about the breakout, let alone assisted in it or planned to help Turner spread some baloney story about The so-called Elders. But she confirmed that he contacted her and asked her to come to a cabin in the woods. She says he didn't say anything about the break-out and she had no forewarning it was coming. He just said there was evidence in the cabin related to his case."

"Was there?" Warren asked.

And Jacob found himself very thankful he'd phrased the question that way. He wasn't ready to discuss Faith's locket yet. He wasn't sure why. After all, Warren must've been fourteen when Faith had died and they'd gone to the same district high school. It's not like Faith's death was a secret to him. Even though they'd never talked about it. Jacob didn't talk to anybody about it. Except his family, if they brought it up first. *And Grace.* He'd opened up to Grace. And now she probably thought he was betraying her. *And I'm not. I'm a cop. A cop first, with a job to do.*

"No," Jacob said. "Nothing related to Turner, the other escaped convicts or the prison break. Turner did accost Grace this morning in the woods and threaten her life. But all he did was repeat his usual lies that The Elders set him up for the crimes he was convicted of. Now, he's also accusing The Elders of being behind the prison break and trying to kill Grace."

Warren just gaped. Jacob didn't dare look at Grace. He felt like he'd let her down somehow—and he probably had—but what other choice did he have?

"All true," Grace said, before Warren could ask. Jacob glanced her way. Her hands were propped on her hips. That incredible fire that was like a mix of guts, determination and courage flashed in her eyes. "I got a letter from Turner claiming there was evidence that he was set up in a cabin in the woods. My boss, Olivia, has been bugging me to take time off and I like camping. So I thought if I was going to take a couple of days in the woods, I might as well try to visit the cabin and see what was inside. I'm curious like that. I found nothing in the cabin."

Jacob noticed she carefully left out whether or not *he* had found anything.

"Turner got the jump on me this morning," she went on, throwing down her words like a hockey player shedding her gloves. "I pulled a gun on him—the gun you just made me surrender—and Turner ran. For the record, Turner now claims he never sent me the letter but that The Elders set him up for that too. I had no idea about the prison break before I went on this wild goose chase, because I'm not dumb enough to go roaming off into the woods alone with three killers on the loose."

She rolled her shoulders back and tossed her head. Neither man spoke.

"Now, I know you've got a lot more you guys want to talk about," she added, "but I'm about ready to get out of these woods. Especially if I'm going to now be questioned by police when I get home. So, do we wait here for a rescue helicopter? Or do we want to canoe to my car? My SUV is parked at the southwest parking lot. Because of how the river's swollen, it took us a lot less time to reach the wreckage than I was expecting. Judging by the speed of the current and the fact that there's three of us, it should be an hour. Maybe less, if it turns out the water's risen so high that we can skip some of the portaging."

Only then did she stop talking and silence fell, punctuated only by the rustle of the trees and the sound of the river flowing by. She was angry. Sure, she'd reined it in, but he could feel it building under the surface of her words. He didn't blame her. He was frustrated too.

Beyond frustrated.

"No, a rescue helicopter's not coming," Warren said. "Because when I managed to get to the radio and call in the crash, they decided to ground the whole fleet until they could be seen by a mechanic crew. First, the entire Search and Rescue crew gets so sick that a whole bunch of people are hospitalized for it. Then the one guy who manages to hop in a helicopter has his bird drop out of the sky and is forced to jump out. So, yeah, everyone's grounded."

And these woods were quickly beginning to feel like some bad joke, where everyone who rushes in on a rescue mission just ended up getting stuck there too. This whole situation was ridiculous and had gone on far too long. What had been happening since Jacob had been gone? Search and Rescue had come down with food poisoning. Helicopters had been grounded. His contact Liam's cover had been blown and then he'd been shot.

His sister's locket had been found in the cabin Grace had been sent to by Hal Turner.

God, help me figure out what's going on. Is there some pattern and connection between all these things? Is there something I'm missing?

It felt like he was somehow breathing underwater and everything would be distorted until he could surface again. "Yeah, canoeing sounds great."

Within a few minutes, they were back in the canoe and paddling down the river. The canoe was more stable with three onboard and the river was indeed running faster. Warren took up the stern and Jacob knelt in the middle.

"So, what else am I missing?" Jacob asked after they'd been paddling a while.

"I think you're up to speed on everything," Warren said. "Kevin hovered in the air as long as he could and flew us back on fumes. That night, the storm hit. Massive flooding. Power went down everywhere. Both landlines and cell towers are down. And then everybody on the Search and Rescue team got sick. It was a nightmare. The last thing we need is to be short-staffed in a crisis. As soon as the airport reopened, RCMP and military started flying in from everywhere to help."

Yup, that matched what Trent had said. Sounded like he was returning home to chaos. But at least for him, chaos was business as usual and part of what he's signed up for when he joined the RCMP. He couldn't imagine what Grace was thinking, knowing she was going to be facing police questioning. His eyes traced down the lines of her shoulders and along her back. She hadn't turned around to glance his way once since getting into the canoe, leaving him staring at the back of her head the entire journey.

He couldn't begin to get his head around why she had done what she had. Why had she come to the woods alone when she got Turner's letter? Why hadn't she told Jacob sooner? Why hadn't she called out to him for help when Turner grabbed her? Why had he held her in his arms? Why had he kissed her? Something in his heart kept pulling him toward her. But it's like he had a stumbling block in his brain.

"…so you'd better be prepared to work overtime for the next few days." Warren's voice cut into his thoughts.

"My brother Trent is getting married tomorrow," Jacob said.

"Oh, right." Warren laughed. "I forgot today was Friday already. I'm Detective Albert's plus one. I guess I'll be seeing you there."

They lapsed back into silence for the majority of the canoe ride, with little more conversation than "Rock to your right" or "Watch out ahead." After a while, a path loomed to their right, and Grace slowed her paddling while Warren steered toward it. Then they pulled the canoe onto the shore and took turns carrying it back through the woods. But still, they barely spoke and the longer they went, the more Jacob realized he missed the sound of Grace's voice. It was amazing how much a part of him—after everything they'd gone through— almost wished that Warren hadn't found them, that they hadn't been growing closer and closer, by each paddle stroke and step, toward saying goodbye. Finally, the trees parted and the parking lot lay ahead. A single black sports utility vehicle sat alone.

He wasn't exactly sure if that was a good or a bad sign.

"That's my car," Grace said. "I figure once we get the canoe loaded up, I'll drive you guys back to Toronto."

Jacob shifted the canoe on his good shoulder and glanced at Warren. "Do you mind giving me and Grace a minute? Maybe you can hang back, make a call and figure out where things are at with Search and Rescue."

Warren's eyes searched his face, but all he said was, "Sure thing."

They set the canoe down, Warren pulled out his phone and Jacob turned to Grace.

"Come on," he said. "Let me walk you to your car. Well, just as soon as I do a quick visual for hostiles."

She nodded. "Go ahead."

He slid his good hand onto his weapon, stepped out into the parking lot and scanned the area. It was empty. He turned back to the forest's edge. Grace stood there alone, looking at him. He walked back to her.

"Once Warren confirms that someone's on their way to pick us up," Jacob said. "I want you to get in your car and go."

He hadn't even finished his thought and already her head was shaking. "No, of course I'm not just taking off and leaving you here, even if the prime minister himself personally assures me help is on the way. You guys can come in the car with me."

"I can't leave this area until the Emergency Response Team gets here, and I can brief them on the fact that Cutter, Driver and Turner are somewhere in these woods."

"Then I wait until they get here," Grace said. "They're going to want to talk to me too. I'm wanted for questioning."

"I know," he said. "That's what I'm trying to protect you from."

He could see her arms about to cross and suddenly he found himself reaching for her hand and to his surprise, she let him take it. Her fingers slid into his, fitting comfortably there in a way that no one else's ever had. He somehow doubted anyone else's ever would.

"Look, I respect your authority as a cop," Grace said, "but I don't need you to protect me."

"I'm not saying this as a cop." Jacob tugged her fingers closer into his. Did she really think he'd be standing here, holding her hand, if he was thinking in the slightest like a cop right now? "I'm saying this as a... friend."

"Friend," Grace repeated the word, as if it sounded as ill-fitting to her ears as it did to his.

And sure, the word didn't seem to quite work and fit the situation, and the way he felt about her, but what other word was there?

"Yes, friend," he repeated. "As your friend, who also happens to be a cop, I'm reminding you that being wanted for questioning by law enforcement is not the same as having a warrant out for your arrest. And while I'm sure the police have a lot of questions for you—" *And I still have questions for you...* "—you're still entirely within your rights to wait. You've spent over twenty-four hours stuck in the woods and once the cops start questioning, you have no idea how many hours they're going to want to keep you. You're exhausted. You're sore. Go home. Turn off your phone. Have a long bath and a few hours of sleep. Then talk to your boss, call your newspaper's lawyer or another lawyer you know. And then go talk to the police when you're refreshed and ready, on your own terms."

She laughed, and he wasn't sure why. It's not like he'd said anything particularly funny. It was more like the kind of relieved chuckle he'd heard slip fellow officer's lips when they'd just survived something traumatic and realized the danger was past.

"Thank you. That…that's not what I expected you to say."

Yeah, him neither.

"Look, if Turner contacts you, report it to the police immediately," he added quickly. "Don't go running around by yourself, trying to meet with him. Also forward any relevant messages, letters or communication you got from him in the past to law enforcement immediately. Your lawyer can help with that. I'm definitely not recommending you keep anything from the cops. But you've already technically spoken to an officer about this. And you've gone through a lot. So there is no harm in napping for an hour or two, getting cleaned up and changing your clothes before you talk to the police. In fact, your brain might be sharper if you do."

No laugh this time. But a smile crossed her lips. It was soft and genuine, and inexplicably made him wonder what it would be like to kiss her.

"So, basically you're saying I look pretty terrible right now?" Her free hand brushed along her hairline. "Because believe me, you could do with a shower too, bud."

He laughed, loudly and for real. "No, I can't imagine you could ever look terrible. No matter what life throws at you. Whatever it is you've got, it's not a surface kind of thing."

Her eyes slid away from his face and scanned the parking lot. And he felt heat rising to his face. Why did he keep saying ridiculous things around her?

There was a noise to their right. He turned toward it. A light brown camper van with faded floral curtains pulled out of the woods and into the parking lot. A young man sat in the driver's seat.

"Hey! Hi!" Grace called. She ran toward it, pelting across the pavement and waving both hands over her head, leaving Jacob to run after her. For a moment, he thought the driver was about to ignore her and keep going. Then she leapt in front of it, her hands raised as if trying to stop the vehicle by sheer willpower alone. The camper screeched to a stop. Grace glanced up at the young bearded man at the wheel. "How are you guys doing?"

What was she doing?

Jacob reached her side, but before he could even speak she grabbed his left hand in hers and squeezed it tightly. For a split second he could see a second person in the vehicle, standing behind the driver. She was young, maybe no more than early twenties with wide eyes and long pale hair. He glanced back for Warren and didn't see him anywhere. When he looked back, she was gone.

"Hello! Hey!" Grace stood in front of the vehicle, holding onto Jacob with one hand, and waving the other hand widely. "Do you guys happen to have a phone charger?"

Jacob started to tug his hand away, but instead of her letting go, she slipped her right arm around his waist too and pulled him closer. Her lips slid across his cheek, their furtive touch sending shivers down his neck.

"They're in trouble," she whispered. "Driver is in that camper. He's got them hostage."

ELEVEN

"Driver? Are you sure?" He turned toward her.

"Positive." Her face was so close to his that their noses bumped. Her breath brushed his lips as she whispered. "Thankfully you and Driver never really came face-to-face, and right now you don't look like a cop."

True, he probably didn't look like a cop right now. But what exactly was Grace planning? To lure the young man and woman out and away from Driver? To convince the killer to let them go?

The camper door slammed open to their right. As they turned toward it, he felt Grace's lips brush his in a kiss so quick and light he couldn't tell if she'd done it by accident or on purpose.

"Hey…um… You guys… Sorry… We—we can't help you." The stammering voice belonged to the young man who'd been driving. He was heavyset with an impressive beard covering the lower half of a face that Jacob guessed was not much more than twenty-two.

"You—you guys gotta move…" the young man continued. His eyes darted everywhere but their faces. Oh, yeah, there was no way these two weren't in danger. "We're kind of in a hurry."

"Hi, I'm Grace!" She dropped Jacob's hand and grabbed the door. "We've been here since yesterday and we've just been canoeing. And you are?"

"Anthony... And I've really got to go." His hand pushed against the door.

"Hi, Anthony!" She stepped forward, practically wedging her knee in the door as it closed. "This is my..." She faltered for a moment as if her brain had stalled out on what word to say next. "Jacob. This is my Jacob. I saw a woman in the window. Why don't you and..."

She let the word hang in the air.

"Kiki," Anthony supplied, as if something in the way Grace had paused had tugged the name from him.

"Kiki," Grace repeated. "How about you and Kiki come out and hang? Our cell phone is really dead, so if you could help us charge it, that would be great."

Okay, so if these two were in danger, Grace was doing a spectacular job of trying to get them away from Driver, almost as good as some undercover detectives he'd known. He slid his hand away from Grace and put it into his front pocket, shielding his gun from view while inching his hand closer to the trigger.

"Yeah, man," Jacob said. "I've gotta call my brother. It's super important. He's getting married tomorrow, and my buddy's vehicle crashed, and now I'm stuck out here with no way to contact him."

Anthony glanced back over his shoulder. His face paled. And Jacob's suspicions deepened to certainties.

Help me, Lord. How do I get these two out of this camper and away from Driver without anyone getting hurt?

"Can we come in?" Grace practically leaped up onto

the footboard. She hesitated for a second, then disappeared through the doorway. The door swung toward him. *No! Grace!* What was she thinking? If Driver really was holding two people hostage, then inside the camper was the last place he wanted her to be. "Stop! Grace!"

He stepped up into the camper, kicking the door open as he went. He yanked his gun from the holster.

The door swung closed behind him. He froze.

Both Driver and Cutter stood at the far end of the camper. Cutter's gun was pointed at the blonde Jacob had seen in the window, who he guessed was Kiki. Driver's gun was pointed down the camper in Jacob's direction. He took a deep breath. Three hostages, Kiki, Grace and Anthony, stood between him and the escaped convicts.

"Police!" Jacob said, his gun raised at the two armed killers in the small narrow camper. "Drop your weapons and get down on the ground!"

For a long second, nothing happened. Then Driver began to laugh. It was an ugly laugh that seemed to fill the confined space.

Jacob took the opportunity to step forward, nudging Anthony out of his way until only Grace stood between him and the killers.

"You drop *your* weapon," Cutter said. "We got two guns and three hostages."

Cutter almost sounded tired, which wasn't surprising, considering he and Driver had probably spent the better part of the day and night hiking through the woods. Both were every bit as bedraggled and mud-covered as Jacob felt. He couldn't get a good enough look at either of their heads to see if one of them had been the person Grace had hit with her flashlight.

"Anthony! Run!" Kiki shouted. "Don't wait for me!"

"Yeah, Anthony, go!" Jacob agreed. "I'll save her! You get out of here!"

The door clattered behind him. *Thank You, God!* Sounded like Anthony had been smart enough to made a break for it when he had the opportunity. One less hostage made Jacob's life easier.

The barrel of Cutter's gun jerked toward the door, but before he could think to fire, Jacob's good hand shot up in the air.

"Hey!" Jacob shouted. "If you're just after hostages, how about you let the women go and just take me?"

Jacob took another step forward, pushing past Grace with his arm in the air. For a second, he worried she wouldn't let him step between him and the killers, then he felt her brush against him as she slipped behind him.

Great. Now, just run out the door like Anthony did, Grace, and I'll focus on getting Kiki.

But he didn't hear the door move.

Driver leaned toward Cutter as if to say something he didn't want them overhearing, turning his head just enough to let Jacob see the side of his smooth bald and tattooed head. No gash. Okay, so then Driver hadn't been the one in the cabin. Then again, he hadn't been their prime suspect.

"What's the plan, guys?" Jacob called. "You made it through the woods, saw this camper van, decided to hi-jack it as a getaway vehicle and take two hostages with you for collateral? Problem is, three is a lot of hostages for two guys to handle. I'm thinking one is all you need. And who better than a cop?"

Please let them forget Grace is a journalist.

He took another step forward, passing the seat where Kiki sat. He felt his shoulders broaden, filling the aisle as he placed his bulk between the women and the escaped convicts. If they wanted to get their hands on Grace and Kiki now, they'd have to go through him.

"Come on, guys!" Jacob's voice rose. "Let's think logically. The sooner we settle this, the sooner you can drive out of here."

He very much hoped the Emergency Response Team was on their way and would stop them on the road.

"Drop the gun!" Cutter snapped. "Now! Or I'll shoot!"

"All right!" Jacob called. "I'll toss it!"

He turned back, his eyes met Grace's and she dropped to the floor as if reading his mind, pulling Kiki down after her. He tossed the weapon past her down to the front of the cab. It smacked against the dashboard. He turned back. "Better?"

"Come on!" Grace's voice was low behind him. Not even a breath later, he heard Grace and Kiki crawling down along the floor behind him, as he shielded them from the killers with his bulk.

"Hey!" Driver shouted. His weapon waved. "Stop!"

Driver fired. Jacob threw himself flat against the wall. The bullet flew past Jacob and splintered the camper wall. The door clattered, and he heard someone tumbling through and a relieved Anthony calling Kiki's name. He glanced back. The camper was empty. *Thank You, God.* Grace and Kiki were gone. And he was alone, trapped in a box with two killers, both of whom had guns trained on him.

"All right, guys!" Jacob said. "It's just you and me!"

Unfortunately, his gun was now wedged against the dashboard at the front of the camper. Now, would he be fast enough to get the gun Grace had taken from Cutter out of his ankle holster before they fired? Probably not, but worth a try.

He started to crouch slowly.

"Get up!" Cutter snapped. "Hands behind your head! Now!"

Okay, Lord, now what?

Sudden sirens filled the air, wailing in the distance but growing closer. Cutter and Driver twitched toward the sound. A cacophony of swearing filled the RV. Then Jacob felt a furtive hand pull the weapon from his ankle holster. *Well, guess I wasn't alone after all.* He glanced down into a pair of dark and fathomless eyes. Seemed Grace had taken advantage of the distraction earlier to roll under the table.

He gritted his teeth and whispered. "Go! Now!"

"I know." She crouched up to her knees and pressed the gun into his outstretched hand. "Be safe!"

"You too." He spun back and fired, his first bullet piercing Driver's shoulder, forcing the gun to fall from his grasp. Then Jacob dropped instantly, feeling Cutter's bullet flying past him through the camper. He rolled behind a cabinet, knelt up and returned fire.

"Grace!" Prayer for her safety moved through his breath, replaced by prayers of thanks as he heard the door clatter.

"I'm out!" Grace called. "I'm safe!"

Sirens grew louder. Voices clamored outside the camper now. Jacob fired again, this time catching Cutter in the leg. The killer swore and fell to the ground. Jacob leaped for him, yanking the weapon from his grasp. Then he grabbed Cutter's head and turned it to the side. No gash. Cutter wasn't the man who'd ambushed them in the cabin either.

"Police!" A chorus of voices seemed to fill the air outside at once. "Out now! Hands up! We have you surrounded!"

He glanced out the window. Cop cars poured into the parking lot. Officers fanned out around the camper. Jacob leaped to his feet and raised his weapon toward Cutter and Driver.

"Lie down on your stomachs!" Jacob ordered. "Hands on the back of your heads! You're done!"

He watched as first Cutter and then Driver lay down and raised their hands. *Thank You, God.* It seemed these two would rather return to jail than die in a shoot-out.

"I need assistance!" he called, keeping his weapon trained on them. No way could he scoop up two guns and handcuff two killers one-handed. Seconds later, he heard Warren and two other officers entering the camper behind him. He patted Cutter down and found Grace's wallet in his jacket pocket. Then he withdrew as Warren took charge of arresting Cutter and Driver. He glanced to the dash. His gun was gone.

Jacob stepped outside into the sunlight. Blue-and-red police lights danced through the myriad of police cars filing into the parking lot. Two of the escaped convicts had been captured. Only one remained.

Uniformed officers gathered around in groups, some

he knew as friends, others he knew as colleagues and a few he just knew of. As his eyes scanned the crowd, he felt his chest tighten, searching to see one singular face.

"Grace!" He pushed his way through the people and cars. "Grace, where are you?"

Then his heart stopped. Her vehicle was gone. Grace had left without even saying goodbye.

"Hey!" He turned toward the sea of familiar and unfamiliar faces. "Anybody see where Grace Finch went?"

"Yo!" Anthony ran over to him, awkwardly keeping one arm wrapped around Kiki's shoulders. "Yeah, she left."

"Left," Jacob repeated. "What do you mean *left*? Why didn't anybody stop her?"

Anthony blinked. "We didn't know we were supposed to stop her! Kiki and I were outside the camper. Then Grace ran out with a gun in one hand and our camper keys in the other." Jacob almost chuckled. So she'd grabbed more than one thing on her way out the door. "Then this man was standing over by her car and he called her. She ran over to him, got in the car and drove off. And then this cop ran out of the trees and then all these cop cars flooded in."

And nobody stopped her. His heart raced. No, no, he didn't like the sound of this.

"What kind of man?" Jacob asked. "What did he look like? Where did they go?"

"I don't know," Anthony said. "Old and white, with a beard. Grace told us to run into the trees and not come out until the police arrived."

Hal Turner.

Dread grew up his spine. "Did he have a gun?"

"I don't know," Kiki said. "I think so. And she said to tell you she really, really wanted coffee, like right now."

"Just drive, kiddo." Her father's voice was low in the back seat. The muzzle of his gun pressed through the driver's seat into the small of her back. "Don't worry. I won't hurt you."

Yeah, she'd heard that from him before. When she'd seen him standing by her car and seen the telltale lump of a weapon, she'd known her choices were simple. Leave with him. Or risk him shooting Anthony and Kiki, before joining with Cutter and Driver and surrounding Jacob.

Had Jacob even made it out of the camper alive?

A cop car loomed ahead on her left.

"Don't even think about it, kiddo."

The gun dug deeper into her back. The cop car passed. They must've been passed by about eight or nine cop cars and emergency vehicles since leaving the lot. None had even so much as slowed as she passed, let alone noticed the escaped convict hiding in the back seat.

"Where did you get the gun?" she asked. "And how long have you had it? It's quite the upgrade from the shiv you threatened me with this morning."

"Don't talk like that," Turner said. "I didn't threaten you. I warned you."

"Like you didn't blackmail me either, right?" she said. "You just kept asking me to deposit money in an account for you and told me you'd tell the world I was the daughter of a dirty cop and cop killer if I didn't. Like you weren't involved in bribery, money laundering or drugs. Like you didn't kill two people. Because nothing is ever your fault."

A siren sounded behind them. Seemed one of the cop cars was coming back this way. She looked up but saw nothing except empty road and trees.

"The Elders set me up."

"Jacob says The Elders are a myth."

"And you believe him?" Turner asked. "He's a cop! You know better than anyone that you can't trust cops. You're a reporter, kiddo. You know the drill. Trust nobody, everybody lies!"

She could trust one cop. She could trust Jacob. And somehow she knew that no matter how hard she dug or where she looked, she'd discover that what Turner was saying about The Elders wasn't true. The siren grew louder behind her. She looked up. A cop car was slowly advancing, growing larger in the rearview mirror. A strong broad-shouldered silhouette sat in the driver's seat. Her heart leaped. She couldn't see his face. The man's left hand clutched the steering wheel.

Lord, do I even dare hope it could be him?

"What's the plan, *Dad*?" Would she ever be able to call him that without feeling the taste of irony and anger on her tongue? Her voice rose, hoping he wouldn't notice she was slowing her foot on the gas. "You going to help me write a big article, exposing The Elders? We're going to camp out together, do a lot of research and take down this secret evil organization together?"

Her father cleared his throat. "Actually, I figured you could handle that. I've got to get out of the country and lay low for a while. A friend of mine has a place in the Caribbean that's totally off the grid. You understand."

She did. She understood all too well. "And you need my help to get out of the country? Lend you some money that you'll promise to pay back some day? Smuggle you across the border? Use me to cover for you, like you tried to get me to mislead the cops and destroy evidence for you when I was a kid?"

Her father cleared his throat. "You make it sound so ugly."

"That's because it is."

And she was done hiding the truth of that. Her mind flashed back to Jacob's face, alone in the cabin as he told her what had happened to Faith. Some things, like it or not, were ugly. But like a patch of earth, filled with grubs, that was hiding under a rock, when somebody dug out the rock and exposed it to the sunlight, something could start to grow.

I don't know what You want me to do with my story, Lord. But I'm done hiding it.

The cop vehicle grew closer. The lights flashed, the sirens roared and the driver's side window opened. Jacob leaned out. Hope surged through her heart.

"Pull over!" Jacob yelled. "Now!"

"No," her father snapped, swearwords slipping from his lips as she felt the pressure of the gun barrel release from the small of her back. Grace glanced up to the rearview mirror as her dad rolled the window down. He leaned out and fired at Jacob.

Jacob's windshield exploded in a spray of glass. *Help him, Lord! Please!* His vehicle swerved, as Jacob struggled to keep it on the road. Turner fired again. Jacob couldn't fire back, not while driving and not with a wounded arm. And she knew he would never fall back, not while she was in danger.

Grace pressed the brake and yanked the steering wheel. Her car spun. Her father swore, the words mingling with the sound of her tires screeching and the sirens growing louder. A blur of blue, green and brown filled her eyes. Then she felt the right side of the hood smack against something so hard the entire car shook. She fell back against her seat. They'd hit a tree. Not hard enough to deploy the air bags, but still lights danced before her eyes. Her head swam.

Help me, Lord. I think I'm going to pass out.

"You crashed the car?" her father shouted. "What's the matter with you!"

I had to. Because if I hadn't, he'd have killed Jacob.

The door flew open behind her. She looked back in time to see her father stumble out of the back seat.

"Stop!" She shoved the car door open and tumbled out. She forced herself to her feet and ran, ignoring the dizziness in her head and jarring pain in her limbs. She yanked the weapon from her belt. "I said stop!"

Behind her, she could hear Jacob forcing his car to a stop and leaping out. "Grace! Wait!"

No, not this time. This time, she wasn't letting her father get away.

"Stop!" she shouted. "Please! Or I'll shoot!"

Her father didn't even pause. She aimed for the air above her father's head and fired. Her bullet split the leaves over his head. He stopped suddenly and looked back. His mouth gaped. "You shot at me?"

"Yeah," she said. "I'm sorry. But I will shoot at you again if I have to."

"No, you won't." Turner shook his head.

He turned to run. She gasped a deep breath, set him in her sites and fired. He shouted in pain and fell. She ran for him. Blood poured from his leg.

"You shot me! You actually shot me!" He swore. "You worthless, useless child! I expected better of you!"

She dropped to the ground beside him, yanked his gun from his grasp and stuffed it into her belt. Then she pulled off her jacket and pressed it against his bleeding leg.

"It was you in the cabin last night, wasn't it?" she asked. "You fired at me and planted the locket."

"It wasn't." Turner's head shook. "I promise you it wasn't."

She leaned forward, grabbed his hat and yanked it off, knowing even as she looked that she'd see the dark red gash her flashlight had left. *And there it was.* "Stop lying, Dad. Just stop lying."

She looked up. Jacob was running through the trees toward them, and every beat of her heart seemed to leap at the sight of him.

"Cover for me!" her dad said. "Cover for me, kiddo, and I'll cover for you."

"No, not this time." She patted him down quickly and when she didn't find another weapon, left him there, bleeding on the ground, and ran toward the detective. "Jacob!"

"Grace!" Jacob reached her side. He dropped to the ground beside her. "Are you okay? What happened?"

No, she wasn't okay. The way her heart was aching, she suspected she might never be okay again. Jacob's hand brushed her shoulder, and somehow the simple gesture filled her with more warmth than hugs from a hundred other men ever could. And suddenly her heart knew. She was falling in love with this man.

And I have to tell him the truth about who I am, Lord. No matter the cost, he has to know.

"Jacob," she said. "I'm sorry. I should've told you sooner. Hal Turner is my biological father."

TWELVE

Hal Turner, the cop killer and dirty cop, the man who spread lies about the police force to cover his own hide, the escaped convict who now lay spluttering, swearing and bleeding from a gunshot on the ground a few feet away from them, was Grace's father? No, it just…

It was true. He looked from the old criminal's face to the strong woman standing in front of him and felt the unanswered questions in his mind start to click into place. Turner was still shouting and swearing, urging him not to listen to her. Jacob tuned him out. A dull ache spread through him, as if his heart had gone cold and was freezing the blood in his veins.

Grace was Turner's daughter. Turner was Grace's father.

"He's the one who was in the cabin last night," she said. "I'm positive. There's a pretty bad cut on the side of his head where I hit him with the flashlight. I'm guessing he didn't pull a gun on me in the woods to keep me from realizing it had been him."

Jacob felt his mouth open. But his throat was so dry he couldn't make a sound.

How could this happen? How could she hide this from him?

How could the first woman who'd ever tugged on his heart be the daughter of a cop killer and a dirty cop?

Who might've killed his sister.

"You're the first person I've ever told," she said. "You're the first person I've trusted enough to tell. He ignored me for most of my young life and wouldn't admit I was his daughter, so I felt too embarrassed to tell anyone. Then when he went to jail, it was easier to pretend he hadn't existed. Then a few years ago, he contacted me out of the blue and started blackmailing me about my identity for money."

She said the words simply and directly, without excuse or embellishment. Her eyes searched his face with a look that asked for nothing more than to be heard. And he believed her. With every painful beat of his heart, Jacob knew she was telling the truth.

"I got a letter from him saying that he'd left proof of his innocence in the cabin and that if I published it, he'd keep my secret," she said. "So I came. It was a really stupid thing to do. But I was scared he'd tell everyone who I was and it would ruin my life. I had no idea about the prison break. Everything I've told you about last night and this morning was true. I just left out that the dirty cop and cop killer…"

"Was your father." Jacob found his voice. "Because…"

"Because I knew once I told you, you'd look at me the way you're looking at me now," she said. "Because I'd kept the secret for so long I didn't know how to tell someone. I just hope you can forgive me."

He bristled. Of course he could forgive her. But gone

was any hope for friendship. Or coffee. Gone too was the way he'd felt building in his chest when he'd heard she'd gone and he'd leaped in a cop car to speed after her, and that unusual way she'd made his heart beat.

It was all gone. It had to be.

He strode toward Turner, pulled his gun and aimed it between the man's eyes. "Did you kill my sister?"

"No!" Turner's face paled. "I didn't."

"Where did you get the locket from? Why did you plant it in the cabin?"

"The Elders sent it to me! The Elders made me do it! The Elders framed me for everything."

Sirens filled the air again now. *Thank You, God...* Jacob started, but somehow the prayer seemed to catch in his chest.

"Stop lying!" Grace looked down at Turner. "Dad! Please! There's no such thing as The Elders is there? I can spend my entire life searching for it, and I'll never find any proof!"

Jacob glanced back. Two cop cars pulled up behind him. Voices shouted. Backup was coming.

"The Elders are real and they're coming for us!" Turner shouted. "You tell them I confessed, okay? You tell them I told you that I did it. I did all of it. I confess. I killed your sister. Accidentally. It was a long time ago. They helped me cover it up, and that's how they caught me in their web. The Elders started using me for little jobs and then they framed me for bigger crimes. But now, I'm confessing everything. I'll confess to all of it. I'm sorry. I killed the girl!"

Jacob glanced back. Cops were coming through the woods towards them. Some he'd worked with and others he recognized. Was Turner really claiming that some of them were The Elders? Or that one of those cops now flooding the scene would pass a message onto a secret group of dirty cops? No, it wasn't possible. Jacob didn't believe it any more than he believed any of Turner's other lies. The Elders were a myth. They were a conspiracy Turner created to cover up his crimes.

Two men in uniform flanked them on either side and one of them called for a stretcher.

"Stop it!" Grace's voice rose, and it took Jacob a moment to realize she was talking to Turner. "Stop lying! The Elders don't exist. You didn't kill Jacob's sister."

"There's a vehicle hidden under a tarp in a storage unit an hour outside Huntsville," Turner shouted. "I can give you the address and door lock combination. When investigator's look inside, they'll find a car with both my DNA and the girl's DNA in it."

"Why are you doing this?" Grace asked. "Why are you confessing to a crime you didn't commit? What could you possibly think you'd get out of this?"

"It's the only way!" Turner said. "The Elders broke me out of jail once. They can do it again! I just need to confess the truth."

No, no. None of this made any sense. None of this was true.

Other cops were stepping between them and Turner now. Warren started reading Turner his rights. Slowly, Jacob slid his gun back into his holster and stood. He stumbled forward through the trees. That feeling of being underwater he'd felt before swept so deep around him it was like he was sleepwalking. He had a confession. Finally, after all this time, someone had confessed to killing Faith. And it all fit.

Then why didn't it feel right?

He hadn't even realized Grace had followed him until he heard her speak his name. "Jacob, I'm sorry."

He turned back. Somehow he'd walked a few paces away from the cops and was now far enough away that they wouldn't be overheard. And there she was, the most beautiful woman he'd ever seen in his life was standing in front of him and it was like something inside his heart was repelling her, pushing her back like an invisible magnetic force, until no matter how close she stood, they'd never really touch.

"Do you think your father really killed my sister?" he asked.

"No, I don't." Her head shook. Tears poured down her cheeks. "I mean, *I can't*. I can't believe he'd ever do something like that. But I know he just confessed. And if he's right about the car..."

He shrugged, and her words trailed off. A criminal was claiming there was concrete evidence. Detectives could check it out. And if it was really all there as Turner said, he would be charged with Faith's murder, and add a third life sentence to the two he was already serving. Did Turner think he had something to gain by confessing? Or the fact he'd broken out of prison once make him think he'd do it again?

"There's a break between the wedding and reception tomorrow," Jacob said. His shoulders rolled back. His jaw set. "Trent and Chloe wanted some quiet family time together, with just the Henrys, before the party. I'll tell my family then. I'll wait until after Trent gets married, then I'll tell him before he and Chloe leave for their honeymoon. Oh, before I forget, I got your wallet back from Cutter."

He reached into his pocket, pulled her wallet out and handed it to her. Their fingers brushed.

"Jacob, I'm sorry I didn't tell you sooner," she said. She stuffed her wallet into her jacket. "I really am. I wish I'd told you. I just didn't know how. You're the first person I've ever told. The first person I've ever wanted to tell. But I was embarrassed, because I really liked you and admired you, and didn't want you to think less of me. And I'm so very, very sorry."

"I'm sorry too," he said. His heart was hurting so badly now he'd have almost wondered if it was physically breaking, splintering and tearing itself apart. "Because I really liked you too! Like a lot. More than I've ever liked anyone. I thought you were smart, and funny, and beautiful, and kind, and interesting, and I really liked the idea of getting coffee with. I liked the idea of kissing you again. But you didn't trust me. And now I can't trust you. And the whole situation is rotten and I wish none of this had ever happened. I wish… I wish Warren had jumped out of that helicopter to rescue you, not me."

A sob slipped her lips, even as her hand rose to block it. Tears slid from the corner of her eyes. But still her chin rose and her shoulders squared. She wasn't cowering. She wasn't backing down. And somehow seeing that cranked the pain in his chest up so high he couldn't even breathe without gasping.

"I don't," she said. "I'm glad it was you and not Warren. Because even if you never look at me or speak to me again, I'm always going to be thankful for every single moment we spent together, even the ones where we were drowning and getting shot at. My life is better, I'm better, because I had twenty-four hours with you."

So was he. He didn't know why or how. He just knew he was too.

Suddenly his hand reached for her face; his fingers brushed along her cheek, feeling her tears pool into his palm.

Why, Lord? Why is the first woman I've felt this way about the one I can't be with? Someone who hid the truth and who hurt me. Someone I can't trust.

One of her hands slid up around his neck and rested there at the nape.

"Goodbye, Jacob," she whispered.

"Goodbye, Grace."

Their lips met. He didn't know or care which one of them had kissed the other first. All he knew is that he was kissing Grace Finch, and that he'd never regret having done so, even as he said goodbye to her forever. Then they pulled apart and she walked away.

Saturday morning sunlight streamed through the top floor windows of the *Torchlight News* townhouse in downtown Toronto. Grace sat alone in the editorial office, leaning forward on her desk and staring at the email from Warren letting her know that yes, authorities had found a car matching the description Turner had given them in the exact location he'd provided. She was thankful the detective had chosen to keep her in the loop, even though she suspected that he was still hoping she'd eventually agree to go out for coffee with him. The words swam before her eyes. Forensics had found traces of blood. They were testing it now.

And if they're a match, what does that mean? That my father really did kill Jacob's sister?

It had been a little less than a day since she'd kissed Jacob goodbye and walked away from him. She'd stood back at a distance and watched as Warren arrested her father, and then he was taken away by a paramedic. A friendly and older cop had then appeared by her shoulder and taken her statement. When she told them she wanted to speak to a lawyer before being questioned further, they offered to help her arrange a tow truck for her car. But despite the impressive dent to the side, her vehicle had turned out to be drivable. She suspected the fact that everything had gone so smoothly was because Jacob had said something to someone on her behalf. But he hadn't spoken to her or even looked her way ever since saying goodbye.

She dropped her head into her hands.

Why do I care so much, Lord? Why did this one man get under my skin this way?

Especially when there were so many more important things to worry about.

There was a creak on the stairs. Her head jerked up. *Torchlight News*'s managing editor, Olivia Ash, stepped into the newsroom, clad in simple jean shorts and a T-shirt, with her long red hair swooped up in a stylish knot at the back of her neck. Grace leaped to her feet.

"Sorry to disturb you!" Olivia held up a hand. "I didn't think anyone would be here. My husband called and asked if I'd pick up a spare camera battery on my way to the wedding. Daniel's camera died during one of the employees' weddings a couple of years back, and since then he has been paying extra close attention to battery life."

"Right, your sister is getting married today," Grace said. She knew that. Along with the fact that as today was Saturday, she didn't really have a good excuse for why she was in the office. Except that she didn't want to be home. She didn't really want to be anywhere. "Your hair looks great, by the way."

"Thanks." Olivia raised her hand as if to touch it and then caught herself. "Chloe, the bridesmaids and I just got our hair and makeup done, then we're changing into our dresses up at the Shield Estate. It's a huge place near Huntsville, with stables, a pond and a small airfield. I think six weddings will be going on tomorrow in various parts of the buildings and on the grounds."

"Well, I hope you have a wonderful day," Grace said. "The weather is definitely gorgeous. Not a cloud in the sky."

She sat down back at the desk and turned her chair toward the monitor, not really reading any of the words on the screen.

For a moment, Olivia hesitated. Then she pulled a chair out from another desk, rolled it over to Grace and sat. "Do you want to talk?"

Yes. But that's hardly fair to ask.

"You have a wedding to get to." Grace shook her head. "Your sister is getting married. You're the maid of honor. You've got your husband, and your daughter, and an entire wedding to worry about."

"Abigail is with Daniel and my parents," Olivia said. She smiled. "Daniel runs an elite private security firm and can definitely handle a preschooler. My sister, Chloe, has organized full-scale emergency rescue team operations to infiltrate organized crime. Trent, the groom, is a detective. His two younger brothers, and groomsmen, Nick and Max, are military and paramedic. And as you know, his best man, Jacob, is a detective. The wedding party and guests combined probably have enough tactical power to evacuate a small country. So, I'm sure my arriving ten minutes later than expected isn't going to cause a major disaster."

Grace laughed and was happy for the break from the tension in her heart. She'd forgotten sometimes at what a power couple Olivia and her husband were. Both were a force to be reckoned with in their own right. But in a way that seemed to make them both shine. She wondered if it had always been as easy as they made it look.

"Thank you," Grace said, not really knowing what else to say. "I really don't like asking for help. I don't even know how to do it right. And I know I shouldn't even be here on a Saturday. But I couldn't sleep and my apartment just felt too small."

"I spoke with our lawyer last night after you and I got off the phone," Olivia said. "She's on deck to go with you for police questioning on Monday. I believe she arranged it with the local precinct for three. We can make a time on Monday to go over anything you want to go over. Also, I'm happy to go with you to the police station as well if that helps."

"Thank you." Grace rubbed her fingers against her temples. "I need to tell you something, and I'm really worried about what's going to happen when I do."

Olivia nodded. "Okay, I'm listening."

"Hal Turner is my biological father," Grace said.

Somehow saying it for the second time was easier than the first.

Olivia nodded. "Thank you for telling me. I'm sorry for how hard things must've been. I can't imagine the weight on your heart right now."

Okay, Olivia hadn't so much as raised an eyebrow, let alone leaped to her feet in shock. She knew? But how? Grace's heart began to race. Grace hadn't told her. If she had, she'd have remembered. "You don't look surprised. Why don't you look surprised?"

"Don't worry." Olivia leaned forward. Her hand brushed Grace's arm. "It's going to be okay. Your life and how you handle it is your business, and I've got your back. You remember Vince, obviously, the old managing editor who hired us both? He covered a lot of crime scenes as a reporter over the years. Took a lot of notes. Took a lot of pictures. A few years back, when he was diagnosed with cancer, I was helping him sort through his life's work in preparation for retirement, and I came across some picture from the day Hal Turner was arrested. He'd managed to snap a couple of pictures of a teenage girl and made a note that a waitress said her name was Grace."

Grace's words to Jacob filled her mind, how journalists know more than they report.

"Vince saw me looking at them," Olivia went on. "He told me a wise pastor of his had told him once that when it came to other people's lives, *Believe nothing you hear and only half of what you see* and that we didn't traffic in gossip. Ever. He said people had the right to tell their own truths on their own terms, when they're ready without being pushed. Then he put the pictures through the shredder."

Thankfulness swelled in Grace's heart. The words she'd spoken to Jacob yesterday filtered through her mind. *We don't ever report anything without proper verification, and in some cases authorization. But that doesn't mean we don't know an awful lot more than we let on.* And yeah, she hadn't been ready to let that be known before. She might not even be ready now.

"Turner has been threatening for years to tell the world I'm his daughter." Sudden tears filled her eyes. "What do I do if he does?"

"I don't know," Olivia said. "But whatever you decide, we're here for you. I know an amazing therapist who might be able to help you sort through it. I can set up an appointment for you. Think of it as having one person you can be totally honest with, about everything."

"Thank you," Grace said again. "I've started praying again. And I haven't for years. I'm not sure what to make of it. Also, I think I'm falling pretty hard for an incredible man who won't even look at me."

"It's going to be okay," Olivia said. "I don't know exactly how or when it's all going to work out. But you're strong, you're a great reporter, you have a good heart and, however you choose to handle this, you're not alone."

Olivia stood, Grace did too and the two women hugged for a long moment.

"I've got to go," Olivia said. "I won't have my phone on during the wedding and reception, obviously. Trent and Chloe requested a phone-free wedding and reception and asked everyone to let their work know they won't be reachable for a few hours and to set up a network of emergency contacts to take their place. And considering pretty much everyone there spends 24/7 tied to their phones, it seemed like a pretty reasonable request." She laughed. "Honestly, I think for some, agreeing to go off the grid for a few hours like that was the biggest wedding present they could give."

Yeah, Grace could see that.

"But if you leave me a message, I'll call you back after church tomorrow. And if you want to spend more time talking on Monday, we can do that," Olivia said.

"Thank you," Grace said, wondering just how many times she'd end up repeating those two words before life fell back into something that felt close to normal. Her phone buzzed. She glanced down. Her mother was calling. She put it through to voice mail and sent a quick text saying she'd call her back in five. "I've got to go and so do you. I'll see you Monday."

Olivia nodded. "You going to be okay?"

"I think so." Grace nodded. "I just don't know what to do."

"In my experience," Olivia said, "as someone who knows what it's like to have your life turned upside down, do your job, be you, focus on what you're good at and the person you were made to be. Also, don't stop praying."

Grace's phone buzzed again. Her mother had texted her back. She said goodbye to Olivia, then waited until she heard her walk down the stairs and out the front door before calling her mom back.

Her mother picked up on the first ring. "Hey, Gracey."

"Hey, Mom." Grace dropped back into her chair and turned to the screen.

"I'm sorry I didn't call you back sooner." Her mom sounded tired, but good. "I just got off a twelve-hour ER shift."

It never ceased to amaze Grace that her mother and Frank, both nearing sixty, still put in long shifts as trauma nurses. Grace had put a quick call in to her at the nurse's station the night before, just long enough to hear her mother's voice and tell her that she was home, safe and okay.

Now it was time for the harder conversation. She jiggled her mouse and her computer screen came to life again. "I told you I saw Hal Turner yesterday. Before he was arrested…"

"He called me," her mother said, in that specific, direct, perfunctory tone that only seemed to come out when she was discussing Turner and terminal illnesses. "Last night, from prison. He left me a message."

Grace dropped the mouse. "Why you?"

"He said he wanted to get a message to you and figured I might pick up and you wouldn't." She yawned. "He told me to tell you that you and he were good. But not to touch the money in the bank account because he'd be needing it in future. Apparently, a friend of his has a place in the Caribbean."

And he thinks he's just going to break out of prison again one day and make his way there?

Grace gritted her teeth and whispered a prayer to fight back the urge to say something bad. After everything that had happened, he still only cared about money. Accessing his hidden online bank account was the very last thing she cared about.

"How can you forgive him?" Grace asked. "After everything he's done, after everything he's put you through, how can you possibly forgive him?"

"I don't know," her mother said. "With God's help? By God's grace? There's a reason I named you as I did. Because you were this amazing, incredible gift God had given to me. Forgiveness is a process. You forgive the best you know how, then you forgive again and again whenever the pain pops up in your heart."

Yeah, she'd heard her mom say that several times before. But somehow now the words rang deeper than they ever had before.

"What are you and Frank going to do if people find out Hal Turner is my biological father?" Grace asked.

"The same as we've always done for over thirty-five years," her mother said. "Love each other, love God and love you the best we know how, one day at a time."

Yeah, that sounded like her mother.

Lord, how do I have faith like her? How do I get there? How do I build up my heart and my life to be as strong a woman as she is? She got over Turner's betrayal well enough to build an amazing marriage with a wonderful man like Frank. They faced the whispers and the shame of gossip together, and no matter what, they're going to be okay. How do I ever become like her?

"He confessed to strangling a twelve-year-old girl," Grace said. "When I was about the same age. He led police to evidence in a car. He's going to get a third life sentence for her murder."

"He did what?" Her mother's voice rose.

"He confessed to strangling a child with his bare hands. When I was twelve."

"And how much was he paid to take credit for that?" Her mother snorted derisively. "Because if he's telling a lie that big, there'll be a money trail."

"A lie?"

"A big, huge, ugly lie," her mother confirmed. "He's conning the police, Grace! Yet another con on top of all his other cons. I don't know why he's doing it. But taking credit for killing someone you didn't kill is evil. What a cruel thing to do to that girl's family."

Grace sat back against her seat so hard she felt like someone had physically jabbed her in the solar plexus, knocking the air from her lungs. Turner's confession had been a con? Jacob was about to call a family meeting, at his brother's wedding, to tell them yet another false story full of lies her father had concocted.

The cruelty of that overwhelmed her.

"Are you sure?"

"Of course I'm sure." Righteous anger pulsed through her mom's words, like she was about to take a whole room full of people to church. "Grace, now, Hal Turner has his faults. He's not a good man. But he didn't strangle anyone when you were twelve. Or thirteen. Or now." She sighed. "Even if I thought he had it in him. He doesn't have the grip strength. He was stabbed, badly, in a stupid fight with some of his drug contacts when you were about eleven and it caused serious nerve damage. He couldn't hold anything properly in his right hand for years. He couldn't crumple a coffee cup, let alone apply enough force to kill anyone."

Olivia had just reminded her to do what she did best. Well, she was a journalist. What she did best was looking for facts. Grace's hands flew over the keyboard. She felt her voice shift from daughter to reporter. "How do you know this?"

"He came to my hospital looking for treatment," her mom said. "He needed stitches and tried to talk me into giving him pain medication. He kept coming back before he was arrested, hoping Frank or I could do something for him under the table."

Of course he had. After everything Turner had put her mother through, of course, he'd still gone to her for help.

"Will there be medical records?" Grace asked. The banking screen opened. She typed her password in and waited. The page loading icon swirled. "Something that someone could subpoena to prove he's lying?"

"Maybe," her mother said. "X-rays could still show the damage. But if he's pleading guilty, investigators might not be all that interested in digging into twenty-five-year-old medical records."

The bank page loaded, and the joint account came into view. Grace let out a long breath as the numbers appeared on the screen. Maybe medical records from a quarter of a century ago wouldn't interest them. But bank records from less than twenty-four hours ago would.

"Someone just deposited fifty thousand dollars into his secret bank account," Grace said. She clicked the deposit. The sender's name was anonymous. There was a message attached to the transfer: *Don't touch, kiddo! See you soon!*

"Somebody paid him to take credit for Faith Henry's murder," Grace said. "By the look of things, he's expecting whomever it is will break him out again so he can spend it."

And she had to warn Jacob.

THIRTEEN

Jacob's phone buzzed in the pocket of his bright red RCMP dress jacket. His hand shot down into his pocket, hoping to catch it before it could fully ring. He cast a quick glance around the upper floor room in the beautiful estate. Members of the groom's side of the wedding party wandered around the room in twos and threes, waiting to head down through a maze of hallways and walkways to the huge refurbished barn where the wedding itself was being held. Thankfully no one had seemed to notice his phone chirp. Jacob reached into his pocket, pulled it out and glanced at the name on the screen. Grace. Again. In the past hour and a half, he'd received about eight texts from the tenacious reporter telling him to call her and about six missed calls. He hadn't called her back once.

A swift hand grabbed his wrist before he could slide his hand back.

"Don't let Trent catch you with that." His brother Nick's voice was low in his ear. Jacob turned. The youngest of the four Henry brothers was standing beside him with a not-unimpressive grip on Jacob's one good arm. At least Jacob's other arm was out of the sling now, bandaged up and usable enough that he'd even been able to ride his motorcycle to the wedding. Unfortunately, his little brother was frowning. And it took a whole lot to make the perpetually upbeat family joker lose his casual grin. Twenty-five years old and a corporal in the Canadian military, Nick had recently reunited with his high school sweetheart and become a father to the son he never knew he had. If Jacob were honest, there was something almost sobering about seeing someone he'd felt responsible for all his life grow up so fast.

"I'm only checking it." Jacob bristled. "I'm not calling her back."

"You shouldn't have it on you at all," Nick said. He dropped his hand from his brother's arm, and then crossed his arms over his chest. "We all agreed to lock our phones in our cars or leave them at home."

"I rode my bike here," Jacob said, sliding his phone back into his pocket. Nick didn't crack a smile. "What's going on?"

Nick gestured him over to the farthest corner of the room, and Jacob had the unsettling feeling that his little brother, the one who he'd babysat and bottle fed, taught to walk and ride a bike, was about to give him a talking to. Or try to, anyway.

"Look," Jacob said, before Nick could get a word in edgewise. "I know I promised I wouldn't have my phone. I'll put it away and I won't look it again."

Had Nick forgotten which one of them was fifteen years older than the other? He felt his shoulders straighten and remembered what Grace had said about how he unfolded himself sometimes to look larger. She hadn't been wrong. He just hadn't ever been called out on it before.

"Who's Grace?" Nick asked. "Sorry, I couldn't help but see her name on the screen."

Oh, no, his little brother was not questioning him about her!

A dazzling, incredible, deep, thoughtful and beautiful woman I almost fell in love with before I stopped myself.

"Nobody," Jacob said. "She's the reporter I rescued."

But Nick acted like he hadn't even heard the words Jacob had said, but had been listening to something else entirely. "If she's so important, why isn't she here?"

"Because Grace is not that important," Jacob said. *She could've been. But she's not.*

"Baloney!" Nick said. "Tell that to the look on your face! She's called you how many times?"

"And I haven't called her back."

"Right." Nick's arms crossed, yet something Jacob could only describe as caring floated in his eyes. "But you can't stop checking your phone. You can't even say her name without going red."

Trent had accused him of that too once. Jacob shook his head. Was this how he'd sounded every time he'd pulled one of his brothers aside for a talk? Loving but infuriatingly hard to shake?

"What is going on with you?" Jacob asked. "Our brother is getting married in less than twenty minutes."

"I know," Nick said. "But something's up with you. You can't stop checking your phone. You're distracted. You told us all we need to have a family meeting before Trent and Chloe leave on their honeymoon. You're my brother. I love you. I want to make sure you're okay and I don't want it impacting today."

No, he wasn't okay. Before he'd reached the wedding venue, he'd gotten the news that Turner's tip-off about the car had been correct. The responsibility of that news, Turner's confession and the fact that he'd found Faith's locket and it was now with forensics was weighing heavily on his shoulders, and how he was going to break the news to his family later.

"Don't worry about it," Jacob said. "I'm your big brother. I've got it covered."

"Yeah, no," Nick said. "You know full well that if Trent, Max or I were in trouble, you'd be the first one rallying the troops to do whatever it took to make sure we were okay. We're there for each other, thick or thin, that's who we are. There are no *big brothers* and *little brothers* in this family anymore. There are just brothers—and sisters-in-law, and parents, and nephews, and probably one day nieces too." A grin crossed his face. "You did a really great job leading us for a long time, bro. You saved all of us more than once. But we don't need you to head the team. Not anymore. We've got your back and we're all in this together."

"It's time!" their brother Max shouted from the other side of the room. "Let's go get Trent married."

Jacob glanced at Nick, feeling he should say something but not sure what. "Thank you."

"No problem." Nick clasped him on the back. "And after the wedding, you're telling me about Grace, and I'm not taking *no* for an answer."

Jacob wished that was all he had to tell Nick about after the wedding. But he set a smile on his face and followed Trent, Max, Nick and his parents through the beautiful old estate and then a tunnel, across a covered walkway and into a huge stone barn. He waited while his father and mother went up the aisle together. Then the four brothers walked to the front of the church, single file. Two hundred wedding guests lined the barn on either side. Flowers spilled from every corner and dazzling lights draped from the ceiling. The Trillium College band sat up front to the side, along with several college students Trent and Chloe had met when he'd gone undercover as their hockey coach. The ensemble was playing a beautiful instrumental piece Jacob slowly began to realize was the *Hockey Night in Canada* theme.

He grinned at Trent. His brother chuckled.

The four Henry brothers stood at the center of the barn, in front of the pastor of their family church. The music changed to the "Wedding March" and he looked up as first Nick's wife, Erica, then Max's wife, Daisy, and then Chloe's sister, Olivia, walked single file down the aisle in flowing dresses of various shades of blue. Then finally, Chloe herself came down the aisle in a flowing white gown trimmed with blue trailing flowers and a navy cape the same shade as her Ontario Provincial Police uniform.

Jacob's heart swelled. *Thank You, Lord, for today. Thank You that You brought Trent and Chloe together. Thank You for all the awesome things You've done in my family's life.*

Trent reached out and took both of Chloe's hands in his. The pastor began the ceremony. Jacob stood at the front and listened to the comforting Bible verses and familiar words as they flowed over him. Nick's words floated at the back of his mind. The weight of the news about Faith sat heavy on his heart.

My brother is getting married, Lord. My sister's killer has been caught. For so many years, my entire life has been about taking care of my brothers and catching my sister's killer. Now that those doors are closing, who am I now? What am I living for? Who am I about to become? What do I do with my life?

A flicker of yellow at the back of the church made him glance up. Grace stepped through the back door of the church, in a simple knee-length dress the color of sunlight and her hair tied back at her neck.

What is she doing here?

She looked up. Her eyes met his. And suddenly he felt everything else, the wedding, the pastor's words and the crowd around him melt away.

And his heart knew without a doubt what it wanted to do. He wanted to run down the aisle, take Grace in his arms and tell her he was sorry for what he'd said yesterday. He wanted to admit that he liked her. No, more than that, he wanted to admit he was falling in love with her. He wanted to ask her out for a coffee today, and tomorrow, and the next day, until they're entire lives were a tapestry of moments spent together.

Still he stood there, helpless, his feet rooted in place at the front of the church and his eyes locked on Grace's face. She hesitated, as if looking for a seat. Then as he watched, Warren rose from the back of the church and walked over to her. Warren's hand landed on Grace's shoulder. They exchanged words, so hushed that even those in the back row of the church didn't turn around, and although Jacob couldn't make out their voices, there was no mistaking the look that crossed Grace's face as Warren stepped closer to her side—fear.

She glanced back at Jacob. Helplessness pooled in her eyes, even as her chin rose. Then Warren half steered and half pushed her back through the door. They disappeared through the doorway.

"Do you, Trent Henry, take Chloe Brant to be your lawfully wedded wife, to have and to hold…"

The pastor's words thrummed at the edge of Jacob's mind. His heart thumped as his mind struggled to process what he'd seen. Grace had walked into his brother's wedding and Warren had walked her out. Why? For disrupting the wedding? No. There was no mistaking the fear in her eyes.

"I definitely do," Trent was saying behind him.

"And do you, Chloe Brant, take Trent Henry to be your lawfully wedded husband—"

Jacob's phone buzzed and then began to ring in his pocket, the loud tinny sound filling the barn. Two hundred eyes turned and locked on his face. He reached for it and glanced at the screen.

Grace.

His eyes rose to the ceiling. The ringing grew louder in his hand.

Lord, I'd better be right about this. Because either way I'm never living this down.

He glanced at Trent. His brother's eyes were on his face.

"I'm really, really sorry, bro," Jacob said. "But I've got to take this."

* * *

"Just keep walking," Warren said. One large hand steered her by the shoulder. The other pressed into her side through the pocket of his suit jacket as he propelled her out of the building and across the field. "We're just going to go have a little talk and sort this all out."

Help me, Lord!

When Warren had approached her in the back of the church, she hadn't thought twice about telling him why she was there. She'd whispered quickly that she had proof Turner hadn't killed Faith Henry and had to let Jacob know as soon as the wedding was over. And the detective had pressed a gun into her side and told her she was coming with him.

She felt her phone ringing in her pocket as it tried to reach Jacob's phone, if that was even the button she'd managed to push when she'd slid her hand into her pocket and tried to hit redial. Jacob hadn't answered a single call or text since she'd found the deposit in her father's account and realized someone had bribed him to take responsibility for Faith's death. Jacob's phone probably wasn't even on.

She felt the vibration in her pocket stop. She prayed that the phone had clicked through to voice mail.

"What's going on, Warren?" she asked loudly, pushing her voice through the fear. "Where are you taking me? Why are you pointing a gun at me? What does this have to do with the bank records I have, proving Hal Turner was paid for his fake confession? Let me go!"

"I can't do that," Warren muttered. He wasn't even looking at her. "Not yet. Not until we go have a little talk."

They were walking so fast she almost had to jog to keep up with his strides. His fingers dug deeper into her shoulder. She'd never really realized how big his hands were before. She glanced back. The barn door lay open behind her. They stepped into the parking lot and he propelled her between the cars to a large black SUV. "Get in."

"No." Her head shook. The pain in her shoulder was spreading down her back and up through her neck. The gun pressed deeper into her side.

"We're just going to go for a ride." Warren's gray eyes were ice cold in his handsome face. "You were saying some wild stuff back there in the church, and I want to talk to you about it. You're just going to tell me everything you know about Turner and the Henry girl. And then I'm going to let you go."

Nah, she didn't believe that last part. Not one little bit.

"Just so we're clear, are you arresting me or kidnapping me?" she asked.

"This will all be a lot easier and more painless if you just cooperate." His voice dropped. Menace moved through his tone. His hand moved from her shoulder to the back of her neck and she felt his grip tighten. His fingers pressed into the veins at the side of her throat, blocking off blood flow to her brain. Her head grew dizzy. Dark spots swam before her eyes. She heard the car door open. He pressed her down toward the open door. *Help me, Lord!*

"What's going on?" Jacob's voice boomed across the field toward them. Warren loosened his grip. Grace looked up. Jacob was striding toward them in his red

RCMP dress uniform. He was coming for her. He'd left his brother's wedding and come after her. "Where are you taking Grace?"

Warren's hand dropped from her neck and she almost fell forward into the car. "Hey, Jacob! What are you doing out here? You should be in there! Your brother's getting married!"

"Trust me, I know!" Jacob called. "But what are you doing? Because it looks like you're arresting Grace!"

"Nah, go, go!" Warren said, and she was amazed how his voice turned from threatening to charming on a dime. "We're just going to drive around and talk."

"I'm not going anywhere until you tell me what's going on." Jacob jogged toward them. Another few steps and he stopped just in front of them. "Grace, why're you here? Are you okay?"

Warren took a step away, but still she could feel the faint pressure of his gun move against her back. She braced her hands on the door frame and gasped a breath. *I'm not really sure why I'm here.* Her head shook. But her throat couldn't even form a whisper. *No. No, I'm not okay.*

"Truth is, she seemed a bit off and I was worried she was going to disrupt the wedding." Warren shrugged. "I'm really sorry, man. She walked in the back during the ceremony. I was pretty sure she wasn't on the guest list. I went up to her and asked her why she was there. She said she had to come tell your family that Hal Turner had given a false confession and didn't kill your sister. She's not well. Maybe she's sick, or drunk, or high, or having a bad reaction to medication. The last few days can't exactly have been easy on her. Anyway, she was babbling, and wanted to talk to your family, and just didn't seem in her right mind. I figured the smartest thing to do was walk her out and figure out what she was on about, before she further disrupted the wedding."

Her head was still swimming from the choke. It was like she'd stepped off one of those flat disk playground merry-go-rounds and still couldn't find her balance.

"Grace?" Jacob asked. "Are you okay?"

"Go back inside, man," Warren said. "It's all good. It's fine. I've got this covered."

No... No, please don't go.

"Jacob…he's…got…a…gun…" she gasped.

"Oh, yeah." Warren blinked. He stepped way back, pulled the gun out and showed it to Jacob. "Was this supposed to be a no-weapons wedding? I am so sorry, man. It's a habit. You know how it is."

She stumbled back from the car. Blood was slowly returning to her brain, like she was waking up solely from a dream. She opened her mouth but her brain stalled. What could she say? Warren sounded reasonable. She'd sound ridiculous. She'd crashed a wedding! And why? To convince the best man not to tell his family they caught their sister's killer? The police had a sworn confession and a car. All she had was her mother's story and a screenshot of her bank account. Jacob had made it clear he didn't trust her. He didn't want her in his life. He didn't want her.

But he'd run out of his brother's wedding for her to make sure she was all right…

Do your job, be you, focus on what you're good at

and the person you were made to be. Also, don't stop praying.

"Grace?" Jacob took another step forward, wedging himself between her and Warren. "What's going on?"

"I don't know who killed your sister, Jacob." She turned her head and looked up at the soft green eyes and generous smile of the strongest man she'd ever known. "I wish I did. But I don't."

"Come on, let's go," Warren said. He stepped toward her. His hand reached out. "You gotta get back in there, Jacob, and she doesn't know anything."

"I don't have the complete picture." Grace stepped back. "But I have facts."

"No," Warren said, "you have a far-fetched theory—"

"Then here's a fact. Turner has too severe nerve damage in his right hand to strangle someone," Grace said. She turned to Jacob.

Jacob's eyes were locked on her face. He was listening. As she watched, something moved through his face that went deeper than sheer compassion—trust. He was choosing to trust her. And everything inside her wanted to throw her arms around him and feel his arms around her.

"Do you have proof?" Jacob asked.

"I have a witness who will attest to that," she said.

Warren sighed loudly. "Witnesses can be bribed…"

"And here's another fact." Grace spun toward Warren, feeling stronger by the moment. "Turner received a lump cash sum of fifty thousand dollars into a secret bank account within hours of his arrest."

"Anyone could have access to that." Warren's neck

and shoulders twitched like she'd just run her fingernails down a chalkboard. "You have access to that."

"You're not even trying to listen to me." She took a
step back. "In fact, unlike Jacob, you forced me out at
gunpoint and *choked* me."

"That true?" Fire flashed in the depths of Jacob's
eyes. "Warren, did you hurt her?"

"No!" Warren said. "Of course not! Jacob! I used
reasonable force in escorting her out and encouraging
her to get into the vehicle. She's got some wild ideas."

No, no, she had facts. Little pieces and scraps of information. Things she could take and build brick by
brick. A cold chill spread slowly down her arms.

"Here's another fact," she said. "Turner only confessed to killing Faith after you and the other cops
showed up. He could have been making sure that you
heard him confess. You could have been the one who
helped him escape prison the first time. He could've
been counting on the fact you'd help him escape again.
You could've been responsible for the mysterious poisoning illness at the Search and Rescue base. After all,
you were there. You could've faked the helicopter crash
and leap to safety. Maybe to keep the other helicopters
grounded so no one would find us too quickly?"

Warren glanced to Jacob. "You going to jump in
here? You going to stop this?"

Jacob paused. His eyes glanced from her face to
Warren's, then back to hers again.

"No," Jacob said. "I don't know where she's going
with this. But I want to hear her out."

*But where am I going with this, Lord? What do I al-
ready know? What do I need to see?*

"You were fourteen when Faith died, weren't you, Warren?" she said. "You lived in that area."

"I was fourteen! I didn't have a driver's license!"

"That doesn't mean you didn't drive a car!" Grace said. "Lots of stupid kids drive around without a license, especially in farm country. You left Ontario shortly after that. You're in the RCMP. You had the kind of access needed to destroy any trace of the DNA evidence found at Faith's crime scene. You had the kind of reach to be able to help facilitate the prison break."

"And made sure that you and I were the ones who searched that part of the woods," Jacob said slowly. "And you transferred back to Ontario after an undercover cop started digging into missing cold case files. And you had the kind of access to know the undercover detective I was meeting with, who then got made and shot."

Warren threw his hands up in the air. "Look, I don't know where you're going with this," Warren said. "But she's lying and because of whatever connection you have with her, you're getting all swept up in her nonsense. When clearly you have somewhere far more important that you need to be."

"Do I?" Jacob stepped closer, until she could feel him standing beside her. His shoulder brushed hers. The warmth of him filled her core. "Because the way I see it, I have a civilian claiming she was assaulted by a police officer who may have attempted an illegal arrest at best and at worst, false imprisonment."

"Really?" Warren stepped toward him. His chest puffed out. "And what are you going to do about it?

Arrest a colleague and buddy? Call in backup at your brother's wedding?"

"If I have to," Jacob said. Her hand brushed against the back of Jacob's. His fingers reached for hers and squeezed them tight like a man who was afraid of tumbling over a cliff. She squeezed him back.

I got you. You've got me.

"Warren, did you have anything to do with my sister's death?"

For a long moment, Warren just stood there, frozen with that wide charming grin stuck to his face like a wax figure. Then slowly, as she watched, his mouth twisted into an ugly grimace.

"No," he snapped. "Of course not."

"You look angry," Grace said, slowly. She turned toward him. "Why is that?"

Come on, Warren, let me interview you. There's a story there, and you're just dying to tell it.

"Maybe because I'm standing here being accused of things I didn't do!" he snapped.

No, it was more than that. There was something deeper there. Her reporter instincts knew without a doubt. She just had to find a way to dig it out.

Grace took a step toward him.

"Are you mad at me?" she asked. His face didn't flicker. "At Jacob?"

No reaction.

Help me, Lord. What question do I need to ask? What do I need to see?

Then the words filled her mind as clearly as if she'd typed them on a screen.

"It's Faith, isn't it?" Grace asked. "You're angry with

Faith. Why? Do you blame her for fighting back against you? For the fact you killed her?"

Warren's fist clenched at his side. His face went white. "Jacob, just turn around and go back into your brother's wedding. Trust me, you don't want to go down this road."

"Why?" Jacob asked. Something hardened like steel in his voice. "Is Grace right? Do you have the gall to be mad at my baby sister?"

"Why?" Warren asked. "Because your little sister was perfect? Because your family, our school, our friends, the media and the entire world decided to mourn her as an angel? What if you're wrong? What if twenty-four years ago, some foolish fourteen year-old boy went on a silly joyride in a stolen car. Maybe he was a nice guy, so when he spotted a girl he recognized, pulled over and offered her a ride. Then she went nuts and started attacking and scratching him. She was out of line. He defended himself and she accidentally died. He then left, put it all behind him, became a hero and dedicated his life to serve and protect. He got hundreds of the worst kind of criminals off the street…"

She could see it all, the tragic events, playing out in his mind.

"You're confessing," Grace said.

"No!" Warren snapped. "I'm just pointing out why Jacob shouldn't believe you. You think I don't know that Hal Turner is your father? Or that you've lied about your true identity for your entire life? Your criminal father is already serving two life sentences and is going to die in jail, anyway." He turned to Jacob. His eyes narrowed. "But if I go down for your sister's murder, hundreds of criminals are going to be able to appeal their arrests, including Cutter and Hunter, who I arrested yesterday. You know what happened when her father was accused of corruption. Can you imagine how much bigger the scale will be if one of Canada's top RCMP homicide detectives is accused of destroying police evidence to cover up a child's murder? Crimes are going to be re-tried. Survivors and the families of victims are going to have to relive their worst traumas. Criminals are going to get out, and some are going to reoffend. People are going to get hurt. Now, do you really want all that on your conscience? Or are you going to do the smart thing, go back to where you're supposed to be and just let Grace and I talk it out?"

The wind brushed the trees. Grace's heart rose in prayer.

Lord, if Jacob's the man I believe him to be, it's not even a question...

Jacob slid his hand from hers. He reached into his pocket and pulled out his badge.

"Detective Warren Scott," he said. "I'm placing you under arrest under suspicion of assault, forcible confinement and murder, for starters."

"Yeah, no! No, you're not!" Warren leaped back. In an instant, his hands rose in front of him. His gun was in his right. A cell phone was in his left. "You think I haven't been setting aside money for my retirement or have a place set up for me to go? I fought really hard to get to where I am in life right now and I'm not going to have you take that from me. That toxin that got every-body sick on base is concentrated, air born and can cause illness so bad it's fatal to children, like your nephews and the elderly, like your parents. There's a handful of canisters hidden around the wedding venue that I set up as an insurance policy. They will go off unless I personally input the code to stop them all. There's no way you can evacuate the entire place before someone is infected. So, I'm going to get in this car with Grace. She's my insurance policy against being followed. Plus, she and I still need to have a talk about who all she ran around telling stories about me to. We're going to leave and go somewhere where you will never find us. When we're clear and gone, I'll deactivate the canisters and everyone will be just fine."

He aimed the weapon between Grace's eyes.

"You've got to decide who you're going to save. Will it be your family? Or Grace?"

FOURTEEN

Jacob stared into the cold dead eyes of the man who'd killed his sister, hurt his colleague, threatened the lives of his family. Then he watched as Warren slid his phone back into his pocket and reached out one meaty hand toward the only woman Jacob had ever let himself begin to love.

Anger filled his heart, coursing over him with a ferocity that momentarily blocked out his ability to think, or pray, or even move. Red swam before his eyes. Blood pounded hot through his veins. *Lord, this man is a monster. And You want me to forgive him? You want me to seek justice instead of vengeance! He doesn't deserve Your mercy. I thought when this moment came I could forgive. But I can't.*

"Jacob, it's okay. I'm going with him!" Grace's voice cut gently and firmly through the chaos raging in his mind. Her hands slid around his neck and he felt the warmth of her body fill his core. "You go take care of your family. I'll go with Warren."

He blinked, the blinding rage fading from his eyes. Grace's face filled his gaze. Her lips brushed his cheek.

"It'll be okay," she whispered. "Go ask Olivia to tell you what she told me about this wedding."

Olivia? The maid of honor? What was she saying?

"No, Grace..."

But before he could finish his thought, her lips met his. He kissed her deeply, pulled her against his chest for one long moment and held her there, as if that's where she was meant to be.

As if that was where they both wished they'd always be.

"Come on!" Warren said. "Now!"

"You'll save them, then you'll find me and you'll rescue me." Grace pulled away. Her hand brushed his face. "Because I have faith in you and because that's what we do. We rescue each other."

"Hey, Jacob!" Trent's voice sounded behind him.

"Dude, what's going on?" That one was Nick.

He turned. The entire wedding party was streaming across the field toward him in an array of flowing fabric, dress uniforms and concern. The door slammed behind him. He turned back. Warren had forced Grace in through the driver's side door and climbed in after her. He watched as Warren pressed his gun into the side of Grace's head.

Grace's words echoed in his heart. *You'll save them, then you'll find me and you'll rescue me.*

Warren's vehicle disappeared down the road through the trees.

"Jacob!" Trent's voice grew louder.

Jacob turned back. His family was halfway across the field. He sprinted for them.

"I think Warren Scott killed Faith," he called, as the

various words he'd practiced on how to tell his family about all that had happened fell from his mind. "Grace and I found Faith's locket in a cabin. Grace's father is Hal Turner and he confessed to Faith's murder. But Grace thinks Warren did it. He just abducted her and basically threatened to kill her, unless she goes along with Turner's confession. There are poisonous gas canisters all around the venue, apparently the same kind that infected people at Search and Rescue, and it's especially deadly for anyone vulnerable like really young kids and the elderly. If I try to stop him, he'll set them off, poison everyone here and kill people. Either way, someone's going to die. I'm sorry I didn't tell you earlier and I don't know what to do."

A pause clicked through the group. He watched lips move in silent prayer and his brothers and sisters-in-law exchange glances.

"Okay." Chloe, Trent's new bride, nodded. "Sounds pretty straightforward. We need to organize the evacuation of the venue. I think Trent can head up one evacuation team. Olivia, maybe you and Daniel can head a second? We'll set up a station to deal with anyone infected and locate any medical staff on site. Max, you got that? Erica and Daisy, go evacuate the day care room immediately. Keep it quiet and calm for now. I don't want anyone knowing we're evacuating until the little kids are out of the building. I'll call it in and organize outside rescue efforts."

Heads nodded. Max, Nick, Erica and Daisy took off running. Chloe reached into a concealed pocket in her wedding dress, pulled out a slim phone and turned it on.

She stepped aside and placed a call, leaving just Trent, Nick and Olivia behind.

"Okay, I did not know she had that," Trent said. "At least she didn't have it on during the ceremony." Trent punched Jacob in the arm. "Go get Grace. We've got this."

Jacob hesitated. "You guys need me."

"Nah," Nick said. "We're good. You raised us well. Go find Grace. Who is she, anyway?"

"A reporter," Jacob said. "A really incredible, beautiful and talented woman."

"She works for me," Olivia added.

"Is she a future Henry?" Trent asked.

"Maybe," Jacob said. "I hope so. Trent? Did you and Chloe actually get married?"

"Yup!" Trent shouted. "We said the I do's and then asked all the guests to stay put."

Jacob watched as his brothers and Olivia turned and started toward the building.

"Wait, Olivia!" he called. "Grace asked me to ask you what you'd told her about the wedding."

Olivia laughed and didn't stop. "I told her we had enough tactical power to evacuate a small country."

"See?" Trent called. "Grace gets it. You go rescue her. We got this."

Warren stared straight ahead through the windshield as he drove, with one hand on the steering wheel and one on the gun he held pointed at Grace. She debated grabbing the steering wheel and trying to crash the car. If she did, would he manage to get a shot off first? If not, would she die in the crash?

Her eyes rose to the rearview mirror, waiting to see the shape of Jacob's car coming after her. They didn't have that much of a head start. He couldn't be that far behind. And yet the mirror remained achingly empty.

"So, what's the plan?" she asked. "If you kill me, Jacob's not just going to pretend that he doesn't know what you did to me or his sister."

"I told you, I have a place." A smirk crossed his lips. "Somewhere nobody is ever going to find us."

Turner's words crossed her mind.

"Let me guess," she said, "it's somewhere in the Caribbean?"

Warren snorted. "Your father told you that, did he? Well, it's roughly in that part of the word, but not as easily located as that. When we get there, you're going to call this witness and tell them not to mention the whole nerve damage thing. Then you'll call your father and remind him to confess. Then when Turner is convicted and everything dies down, I'll let you go."

No, he'd kill her or he'd keep her. But he'd never let her go. Fear and faith beat through her heart in equal measures. "Jacob won't stop looking for me and he will find me."

Warren pulled off the road into a tiny airstrip. A small Cessna Skyhawk sat on the runway.

"Not if he doesn't know what country to look in." He waved the gun toward the aircraft. "Come on. You and me are going on a little flight."

The fear in her chest roared louder. Tears filled her eyes. Her legs shook as she stepped from the car and let him lead her across the airfield. His hand clamped painfully on her neck. The other pressed the gun into her side.

"You promised to deactivate the gas," Grace said.

"I was lying," Warren said. "What better cover for your disappearance than a huge illness outbreak at the family wedding of the girl your father admitted to killing. Now, hold out your hands."

She resisted the order until the pain in her neck grew so tight she thought she was about to black out. He zip-tied her wrists together. Wind brushed the trees. Stillness filled the air. The sound of a vehicle roared toward them, then disappeared in the distance as it passed the entrance to the airfield. Warren opened the door to the small aircraft and forced her to get inside. She climbed into the passenger seat. Her hands shook. He started the engine and the small plane started down the runway. The road behind them lay empty.

Was I wrong, Lord? Am I really all alone? Is nobody coming for me?

An engine roared. She looked up as a motorcycle shot through the trees ahead. A tall man in a red Mountie jacket was weaving his way toward the racing plane.

Jacob!

The plane was picking up speed. Jacob was racing closer. Warren leaned out of the window and fired. Jacob swerved, dodging the bullets as they flew toward him. She couldn't imagine how much pain his shoulder must be in. The plane began to lift. Jacob wasn't going to make it. They were going to take off and leave him behind.

Jacob yanked his handlebars hard to the right as his bike skidded sideways, flying underneath the tiny plane.

His body rolled along the tarmac as he leaped free. A thud shook the plane as the motorcycle hit the wheels. The tail cracked. The plane spun like a Frisbee off the runway and into the trees. Her eyes closed.

The plane stopped. Warren was hunched over the steering wheel, groaning. Jacob was running toward them. Warren raised his weapon and aimed it at Jacob, but Grace punched him hard in the back of the head with her bound hands before he could get off a shot. Warren slumped forward. She pulled the gun from his hand and tossed it out the window.

"Grace!" Jacob called. "You all right?"

"Yes!" She checked Warren's neck. His pulse was strong, and he was breathing. Jacob reached her door and yanked it open. She tumbled out into his arms. "Warren's down. I hit him pretty hard. He's unconscious but breathing. I need help getting out of these zip ties. How's the wedding?"

"My family's evacuating the venue and calling backup." Jacob slid a knife from his pocket, slipped it between the ties and cut her free. Then he lifted her off her feet with his good arm. "You're amazing, you know that?"

"So are you." Her lips brushed his face, then his mouth found hers for a long moment.

Then Jacob broke the kiss and set her down. He climbed into the cockpit, and she watched as he secured Warren's hands and feet with more zip ties he found in Warren's jacket pocket. Then Jacob leapt back to her side.

"We need to get back to the venue," he said, "help with the evacuation and call in for Warren's arrest. I should also call my brother, the paramedic, to look at him." Then he glanced back to the plane. "Remind me quickly what your mother said about forgiveness being a process?"

"You forgive the best you know how," Grace said, "then you forgive again, and again, whenever you need to."

"Forgiving Warren might be a very long process," he said.

"Forgiving my father too."

His fingers tightened in hers. Jacob grabbed her hand and they started jogging back toward the venue.

"Which brother is the paramedic?" she asked.

"Max. It's a big family, but you'll get used to us."

She glanced back at the plane. The remains of his motorcycle were wedged under it. "I'm sorry about your motorcycle."

"Yeah, I really should've bought a cheaper one and saved some money for my wedding."

She glanced at him sideways. "I thought you weren't the marrying kind."

"Maybe not, but I can try to be." His voice deepened. "Because I think I've finally found someone worth spending my whole life with."

Hope filled her chest like bubbles of light, rising up inside her and spilling out into her limbs. "Have you now?"

"Yeah, Grace, I have." His hand tightened in hers. "You're the most extraordinary person I've ever met, Grace. Thank you for jumping from the helicopter ladder to save me. I didn't get it then. But I get it now. I needed you to rescue me, and I needed to rescue you. I know we got off to a rough start, and I know we have a lot of steps to take before we get there, starting with coffee. But I think being together is something worth fighting for."

The trees parted. The venue appeared ahead. People spilled across the lawn. His brother Nick was directing evacuees into groups. His parents, Daisy, Erica and his nephews were gathered by the pond. Chloe stood in her wedding dress and directed emergency vehicles as they arrived. Trent looked up at them from amidst the chaos and waved.

Jacob paused and turned to Grace. "This is my family. This is my life. And I want you to be a part of it. Trust me, this isn't a conversation I want to have right now in the middle of a crisis. But I can't wait another moment. I think I'm falling in love with you, and I just can't stop smiling at even having the hope of spending my forever with you."

"I think I'm falling in love with you too," she said.

Then she kissed him quickly and together they ran into the fray.

EPILOGUE

Snow buffeted gently outside the Henry farmhouse living room window. Red-and-green lights twinkled in from the towering pine tree. The voices of Henrys, old and new, filled the air, spilling over and on top of each other like music. Nick, Erica, their son, Zander, and his cousin Fitz sat on the floor underneath the tree with Fitz's parents, Max and Daisy, squeezed together on an armchair close by. Jacob's father and Chloe were standing by the window discussing crime. His mother and Trent were carrying more plates of cheesecake squares, Nanaimo bars and cookies out to place on the already crowded table. Faith's locket, now back from forensics, hung high on the tree beside the star. His mother's latest painting hung over the fireplace with the words inspired by Psalm 119:90, "Great is thy faithfulness, God, through all generations."

Jacob sat back on the overstuffed love seat, wrapped his arm around Grace's shoulder and pulled her closer into his side. He leaned over and brushed his lips on the top of her head. *Thank You, Lord, for my family, for Grace, for everything You've brought into my life. You have done far more in my life than I ever dreamed. You comforted and healed us when we were broken. You strengthened us for Your work in the world. You brought us together as a family. I can't thank You enough.*

Max and Daisy stood. His arm slipped around her waist and pulled her close. His fingers splayed gently across the side of her stomach. "Before we open presents, we have an announcement to make—"

"No, you don't!" Nick leaped to his feet, with a laugh, before reaching down to help Erica up. "Because we have an announcement too and you're not stealing our moment."

Jacob's two youngest brothers stood for a moment in the living room, staring each other down. Erica and Daisy exchanged a look and a laugh that made Jacob pretty sure they already knew what their husbands were going to say.

"We're having a baby!" Nick and Max said at once.

"With Daisy," Max added quickly. "We're due in June."

"Beginning or end of the month?" Nick asked. "Because Erica and I are due around the second week."

"Third week," Max said.

Nick had barely gotten out half a laugh before Erica poked him in the ribs. "If you try to make our baby a competition with your brother, I'll kill you."

Nick wrapped his arms around her and kissed her. "I won't."

"I won't either," Max said quickly, kissing Daisy.

Then the couples pulled apart as their family rushed in to congratulate them.

Jacob hung back and let the rest of the family exchange hugs first. He bent down and kissed Grace softly. "Welcome to your first Henry family Christmas."

"Hey!" Max raised his head above the crowd. "Does anybody else have anything important to announce? Because we might as well get all the announcements out of the way first."

Jacob glanced down at the beautiful woman in his arms. Light danced in her eyes.

"Maybe," he said. "Give us a moment."

A chorus of laughter rose from around the room as Jacob got up, took Grace by the hand and walked through into the kitchen, thumping both Max and Nick on the shoulders in congratulations as they went. They put their coats and boots on and slipped out the back door. Then Jacob led her around the house, back to the front porch. They sat there on an old wooden swing and glanced through the window at the happy chaos of his family inside.

"If they both have girls, they'll name them both some variation of Faith," Jacob said.

The seat rocked gently. His eyes rose to the sky.

In the months since the prison break, Warren had been charged with Faith's death and a slew of other more recent corruption and bribery charges. Liam Bearsmith had regained consciousness and provided evidence that Warren had destroyed multiple DNA samples and other pieces of evidence during his career in exchange for cash bribes from dozens of criminals. While Warren had both targeted and worked with criminals, like Hal Turner, thankfully there was no evidence any other cops had ever helped Warren with his crimes.

After a long fight on his behalf, Grace's father was

finally getting proper psychological help and had admitted to inventing The Elders, though his need to cast himself as a victim persisted. Grace had written a lengthy op-ed for *Torchlight News*, letting the world know that Turner was her biological father. Social media was cruel at first, but her colleagues and newspaper had stood by her, and then stories began to spill out from people who'd been inspired by Grace's courage to face their own family secrets.

Forgiving Warren had turned out to be even harder than Jacob had expected, but he knew God was working on his heart and he could now see the man's face on the news without feeling a sudden surge of pain. Most importantly, he had Grace standing beside him, sharing his pain and letting him help carry hers. They had been slowly weaving their lives together, with coffees, and walks, and long conversations, going to the gym together after work and church together on Sundays. He'd had so many Saturday family dinners with her mom and Frank he was now an honorary part of the family. Then at the end of December, they'd started going to see Grace's therapist together for couple's counseling, working through their trust issues, their pasts and how to build something strong together.

"When your mom and Frank come back from Florida, I want to get them together with my family for dinner," Jacob said.

"I'd like that." Grace smiled.

He gradually slid his hand into his pocket and pulled out a small red-and-green box. He opened it slowly. The ring was simple, with a golden band and a large diamond solitaire in the middle.

"I hope you like it," Jacob said. "I managed to sell the remains of my motorcycle to a mechanic online. I told him I needed the payment by Christmas and he understood."

He slid from the seat and knelt at her feet in the snow. "Grace Finch?"

Happiness dazzled in her eyes. "Yes, Jacob Henry?"

"I'm in love with you."

"That's good." Her smile grew wider. "Because I'm in love with you too."

"Good." He chuckled. "I spent all week trying to come up with the right words to say. All I know is that I want to marry you. I want to share my life with you. I want to share all my adventures, everything good and bad with you. I want you to be the family I come home to at night. I think I know your heart and I think you know mine, so let's make it official. Will you marry me?"

"Of course." Her hands slid to the side of his face and she kissed him. "I can't wait to marry you."

He tugged off her glove and slipped the ring on her finger. A chorus of laughter, cheers and pounding shook the air. His entire family was crowded up around the window with their hands pressed against the glass to look outside. "Looks like we've got an audience."

"Sounds like I'm going to have to get used to it." She laughed. "I'm looking forward to it."

"Me too."

And they wrapped their arms around each other and kissed deeply, before heading back into the farmhouse.

* * * * *

Dear Reader,

As this summer ended, I was sitting outside on a picnic table, working on the book in the hazy warm night. A man came by and asked me what I was working on. So I told him I wrote books for Love Inspired Suspense and started telling him about the Henry brothers. He told me that he was an RCMP officer and that two of his close friends and colleagues were recently killed in the line of duty just a few days earlier. I folded up my laptop and he told me about his friends—one male and one female officer—what they'd been like as officers, and what had driven them each to serve in law enforcement. Then after a while, he started telling funny stories about the line of duty too, like being called out to rescue a skunk who'd gotten a McFlurry cup stuck on its head.

Thank you so much to all of you who've shared the journey of Jacob, Trent, Max and Nick with me. Something affected me really deeply about these brothers—how their sister's death impacted them, the way they were driven to serve others and the strong, extraordinary women who fell in love with them. I like how they each found healing, purpose, love and faith. I will miss writing about them very much. Thank you so much to all of you who wrote letters to me about these books, especially Nancy Tekulve, who asked me to include Trent and Chloe's wedding, and Merianne Bawden, who asked for an update on Daniel and Olivia.

I'm also grateful for everything I've learned about Canada's military, paramedics and law enforcement through writing these books, and the deeper appreciation I've developed for the work they do. May we always remember to appreciate the real heroes and heroines in our midst.

Thank you so much for sharing this journey with me,
Maggie

COMING NEXT MONTH FROM
Love Inspired® Suspense

Available August 6, 2019

SEEKING THE TRUTH
True Blue K-9 Unit • by Terri Reed

By investigating the murder of the NYPD K-9 Command Unit chief, reporter Rachelle Clark draws a killer's attention. And if she wants to stay alive, relying on the late chief's handsome brother, Officer Carter Jameson, and his K-9 partner is suddenly her only option.

THE CRADLE CONSPIRACY
The Baby Protectors • by Christy Barritt

With someone willing to kill to get to the little boy Sienna Thompson's babysitting, her next-door neighbor, FBI agent Devin Matthews, vows to protect her and the two-year-old. But when they discover the child's mother isn't who she claimed to be, can they survive long enough to uncover the truth?

MARKED FOR REVENGE
Emergency Responders • by Valerie Hansen

When EMT Kaitlin North realizes a gunshot-wound patient is the police officer who once saved her life, she's determined to return the favor. But with a price on Daniel Ryan's head and no one to trust, can she hide him from the hit men?

LOST RODEO MEMORIES
by Jenna Night

After Melanie Graham awakens in the woods with a head injury and no memory of what happened, she quickly learns that someone wants her dead. Can sheriff's deputy Luke Baxter keep her safe as he works to identify the unknown assailant?

SECURITY MEASURES
by Sara K. Parker

To halt a killing spree, bodyguard Triss Everett tightens security at the senior community where she volunteers—and makes herself a target. Her coworker, widowed single father Hunter Knox, won't let her become the next victim. But as Hunter fights for Triss's life, he finds himself also fighting for her love.

INTENSIVE CARE CRISIS
by Karen Kirst

Reporting missing medical supplies and narcotics lands nurse Audrey Harris and her patients right in the crosshairs of a ruthless thief. But when Force Recon marine sergeant Julian is one of the patients in danger, the criminals unwittingly provide her with a strong—and handsome—protector.

LOOK FOR THESE AND OTHER LOVE INSPIRED BOOKS WHEREVER BOOKS ARE SOLD, INCLUDING MOST BOOKSTORES, SUPERMARKETS, DISCOUNT STORES AND DRUGSTORES.

LISCNM0719

Get 4 FREE REWARDS!

We'll send you 2 FREE Books plus 2 FREE Mystery Gifts.

Love Inspired® Suspense books feature Christian characters facing challenges to their faith... and lives.

FREE Value Over $20

In the wake of his estranged wife's murder, widower Michael Forster returns to the Amish community he'd left as a teen, seeking a fresh start for himself and his daughter, Allie, but the past is determined to follow him...

Read on for a sneak peak at
Amish Outsider by Marta Perry,
the first book in the new River Haven series,
available July 2019 from HQN Books.

Cathy looked up again at Michael, to find him watching his child with a look compounded of love, protectiveness and bafflement. Maybe he wasn't finding it easy to be a single dad. Her heart twisted with pity, and she longed to reassure him.

"If she gets upset—" he began.

"Please don't worry about it. She'll be fine. If there are any problems, I'll send someone to fetch you. You're at Verna's house, ain't so?"

He nodded, giving her a bleak look. "News travels fast."

"It's a small town." If he remembered anything about River Haven, he ought to remember that.

"Yes. And people have long memories."

There didn't seem to be any answer she could make.

"I'll be here to pick up Allie at three o'clock. Don't let her leave with anyone else." It was an order, and he followed it by striding out the door.

Michael had gone, but he'd left a turbulence in the air. Or maybe the turbulence was only in her.

She'd heard all the stories about him, and her instinctive reaction had been to believe him innocent. How could someone who'd been raised here, who'd grown up nourished on simple Amish values of faith and family, honesty and humility, possibly have done such a thing?

Now she'd encountered him for herself, and she didn't know what to believe. She had expected to have a sense of the familiarity that linked Amish to Amish. But that hadn't happened. He seemed foreign to her, as if there was no point at which their lives could touch.

Collecting herself, she walked between the rows of desks to the front of the room and picked up the Bible that lay open on her desk, ready for the morning reading. Her gaze lit on Allie, who was watching her with a sort of shy hope in her face.

Cathy's heart warmed, and she smiled. If she looked for a point where their lives touched, it was here in the form of a small child who needed her.

Don't miss
Amish Outsider *by Marta Perry,*
available July 2019 wherever HQN Books
and ebooks are sold.

www.Harlequin.com

Looking for inspiration in tales
of hope, faith and heartfelt romance?

Check out **Love Inspired**® and
Love Inspired® Suspense books!

New books available every month!

CONNECT WITH US AT:

Facebook.com/groups/HarlequinConnection

Facebook.com/HarlequinBooks

Twitter.com/HarlequinBooks

Instagram.com/HarlequinBooks

Pinterest.com/HarlequinBooks

ReaderService.com

Love Inspired®

LIGENRE2018R2

What happens when the nanny harbors a secret that could change everything?

Read on for a sneak preview of
The Nanny's Secret Baby,
the next book in Lee Tobin McClain's
Redemption Ranch miniseries.

Any day she could see Sammy was a good day. But she was pretty sure Jack was about to turn down her nanny offer. And then she'd have to tell Penny she couldn't take the apartment, and leave.

The thought of being away from her son after spending precious time with him made her chest ache, and she blinked away unexpected tears as she approached Jack and Sammy.

Sammy didn't look up at her. He was holding up one finger near his own face, moving it back and forth.

Jack caught his hand. "Say hi, Sammy! Here's Aunt Arianna."

Sammy tugged his hand away and continued to move his finger in front of his face.

"Sammy, come on."

Sammy turned slightly away from his father and refocused on his fingers.

"It's okay," Arianna said, because she could see the beginnings of a meltdown. "He doesn't need to greet me. What's up?"

"Look," he said, "I've been thinking about what you said." He rubbed a hand over the back of his neck, clearly uncomfortable.

Sammy's hand moved faster, and he started humming a wordless tune. It was almost as if he could sense the tension between Arianna and Jack.

"It's okay, Jack," she said. "I get it. My being your nanny was a foolish idea." Foolish, but oh so appealing. She ached to pick

Sammy up and hold him, to know that she could spend more time with him, help him learn, get him support for his special needs.

But it wasn't her right.

"Actually," he said, "that's what I wanted to talk about. It does seem sort of foolish, but…I think I'd like to offer you the job."

She stared at him, her eyes filling. "Oh, Jack," she said, her voice coming out in a whisper. Had he really just said she could have the job?

Behind her, the rumble and snap of tables being folded and chairs being stacked, the cheerful conversation of parishioners and community people, faded to an indistinguishable murmur.

She was going to be able to be with her son. Every day. She reached out and stroked Sammy's soft hair, and even though he ignored her touch, her heart nearly melted with the joy of being close to him.

Jack's brow wrinkled. "On a trial basis," he said. "Just for the rest of the summer, say."

Of course. She pulled her hand away from Sammy and drew in a deep breath. She needed to calm down and take things one step at a time. Yes, leaving him at the end of the summer would break her heart ten times more. But even a few weeks with her son was more time than she deserved.

With God all things are possible. The pastor had said it, and she'd just witnessed its truth. She was being given a job, the care of her son and a place to live.

It was a blessing, a huge one. But it came at a cost: she was going to need to conceal the truth from Jack on a daily basis. And given the way her heart was jumping around in her chest, she wondered if she was going to be able to survive this much of God's blessing.

Don't miss
The Nanny's Secret Baby *by Lee Tobin McClain,*
available August 2019 wherever
Love Inspired® books and ebooks are sold.

www.LoveInspired.com